KB263598

N1E2

Contents

Chapter 01

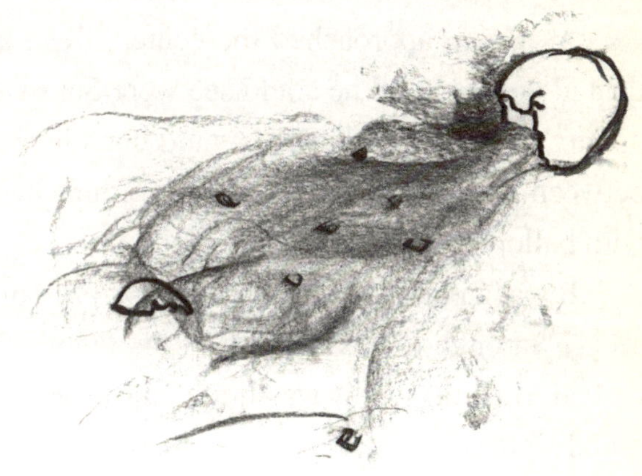

It was the year 2631, the 500th anniversary of the creation of the N1E2. The ground was barely visible as there were thousands of people crowded in the center street of the city. There was a sea of people everywhere, standing along the sides of the parade route and also hovering in the air above, a multitude of Sans dressed all in green.

Everyone seemed excited. Each and every one of the open sea of greenness wore a smile on their face, and all were chanting an incomprehensible song of words calling for the parade to begin. Some were gossiping with the people next to them while others broke out singing the song of the N1E2. This was truly a blessed day, a day in which almost all would be brought together as one. Of course, a few were certainly excluded. Bryan was one of these outcasts.

As Bryan approached the center street, he looked up and down but all he could see were Sans wearing all green. Where the odd space would open here and there between the Sans, it would often be immediately filled with balloons. It was a day of celebration.

It was in fact the greatest spectacle Bryan had ever seen. Although it was not one of his favorite holidays, he had to admit that it was quite enjoyable to see such grand sights.

He had worried he would not be able to see it because of the lack of light but the Sans had prepared portable lamps so that everyone could see the show. In the sky were huge green balloons shaped like injections, and there, one big balloon that was shaped like a doctor wearing a white gown with a stethoscope around its neck.

The streets were filled with green Sans wearing green clothes, holding green balloons, and even more surprising, a smile on their green faces. But hidden among these happy people were no doubt humans like Bryan who were trying to act and dress like the rest in an attempt to be inconspicuous. They surely all had the same thought in their mind, 'If they find me, I'm dead.'

Bryan was relieved that he came wearing his green coat. The green would make it easier to blend in.

Bryan walked around, looking for an adequate spot to view the parade from-somewhere where he wouldn't be easily noticed. He knew that this holiday had the highest rate of human assault so he had to be extra cautious. He hid in the middle of a crowd of people, popped his collar to hide his face and waited for the parade to begin. Next to him was a group of sans not caring who entered the crowd, jumping up and down, cheering.

From where he was standing Bryan was able to spot three other humans, all wearing green make up. It was hard to distinguish the humans from the Sans when the Sans were not flying but there were still ways to separate the two. All Bryan had to do was look for people who were wearing thick clothing that was not appropriate for the weather. It was the middle of the summer but the humans wore coats big enough to hide their faces. The Sans however, were too busy with the excitement to be bothered with human sightings.

Soon the parade began and John Servodeus V appeared, leading a whole line of parade balloons as a live band played his own special anthem in celebration of his arrival. Clothed in an emerald green and sparkling gold robe, he stood tall, seemingly unaware of his five foot six stature. The robe, in all of its ostentatious glory, dragged on the pavement behind him, catching bits of trash and debris as he moved through the crowd.

There were so many fans and visitors that Bryan could barely see him. Spectators were screaming Servodeus' name in such harmony, it seemed as though they were a choir. His orange hair and beard contrasted with his green face and eyes. His face was rather ugly. His high forehead gave him a primitive, ape-like appearance. On the other hand, he lacked a distinct chin because of his obesity. Bryan could never understand how a San, someone that does not have to eat, could get so fat. To Bryan, this man looked like a monster, but everyone else seemed to be blinded by the revolutionary gift the man's great grandfather had bestowed upon the people one hundred years ago.

From what Bryan had learned from his orphanage school, five hundred years ago today, on June 19, 2131, Dr. John Servodeus Jr. had changed humanity forever with an injection that would evolve Homo sapiens into the superior Homo Sanus. At the time, the world was in chaos due to global warming and the lack of an adequate power source to replace the long spent fossil fuels. People had tried relying on hydrogen and nuclear power; only to discover that the two were not enough to satisfy the amount needed, or demanded. One by one, cities were destroyed by demonstrators rebelling against the government for not coming up with a proper solution to this global crisis.

The vaccine, N1E2, would solve all the world's problems. Anyone who was injected with it would gain supernatural abilities. One of the most energy consuming and waste producing problems was transportation but with this injection, cars and planes were no longer needed. The N1E2 injection gave anyone who took it the ability to fly. People became stronger and more resistant to diseases and consequently were able to live longer. There would be less waste in the environment, thus helping to solve the global warming crisis; and more, any taker of the N1E2 vaccine was given the power to photosynthesize and thus did not require anything for sustenance but routine amounts of water and sunlight, which were both plentiful.

Being injected by this drug soon became a mandatory procedure in all parts of the world and soon almost everyone became a member of this new race, the Homo-Sanus. In time, they came to be called the Sans. The Sans were a better, stronger and longer lasting version of humans except for some minor side effects. After three or four years, those who took the drug found that their skin color turned abnormally white, and then green, in addition to there being other unseen problems to this miracle injection. Other than these side effects however, the injection made people godlike. This drug was such a great influence, that Doctor Servodeus was granted his own holiday, one which was celebrated all over the world. John Servodeus V was now at the parade to represent his great-great-grandfather and to bask in his family's glory.

Servodeus waved at the crowds with his long gorilla arms with an arrogant grin on his face, as if he were the one who had invented the drug himself. Behind him was a band of people wearing green. Around their heads were headbands with a green sun emblazoned upon on it. These people were referred to as Sun Worshipers. They were an army of human-hating followers of Servodeus that often resorted to illegal acts of violence against humans. Although Servodeus acted as if he were not responsible for the violent acts of the Worshippers, and claimed to have given no such orders to his followers, the fact was that he had the power to stop these people whenever he wanted, but did not use it. The worshipers treated Servodeus like a god.

Bryan sensed that the worshipers he saw had not come to the event with a clear mind. They had probably been drinking or doing drugs. Although food was not necessary for Sans, alcohol and drugs were still available in the markets, strictly for their use.

These mind altering products were considered a luxury that only evolved people were qualified to have.

Just then, an egg was thrown at Servodeus along with a nasty comment.

"You ape!" a man shouted angrily at Servodeus. That was the first time Bryan had heard someone say that out loud. But he had always thought it himself.

The egg did not hit Servodeus but it did anger the Sun Worshipers. Suddenly a dozen Worshipers flocked toward the direction the egg was thrown from and found the culprit. Bryan could not see him but he could hear the man screaming for help and mercy. The initial courage the man had boasted when throwing the egg had disappeared completely. The sun worshipers beat the man savagely, kicking and spitting at him as he lay curled up on the ground. Then, picking him up like a doll, they threw him onto the street and began kicking him some more. Bryan could not see the actual beating but he could see the smirk on Servodeus' face as his followers destroyed the powerless man. Bryan looked around, hoping to see someone stand up for the man, but no one moved. They were all as scared as he was.

As he watched helplessly, Bryan found his mind seeking escape from what was taking place before him. Strangely, he thought about how expensive eggs were at the specialty store. Eggs were so highly priced because of the limited supply of chickens. Most were now used for cloning and other scientific purposes. Few were left for producing eggs. Because Sans did not need eggs to survive, the government saw little point in saving the chicken population and there was very little profit to be made in chicken farming.

As Bryan pondered on about the egg, the person who had thrown it in the first place was half dead in the street. No one came to help the person up, nor did any police arrive. This was because the Sun worshipers were the government. This simple truth had great impact upon Bryan's life. The Sun Worshipers attacked humans all the time but not even the other Sans, who were definitely strong enough to stop them, ever attempted to help.

Because these days almost everyone had received the injection and now could do everything without assistance, it had become the new ethic that everyone had to and should tend for themselves. This was why all newborns were sent to orphanages, the children of Sans and humans both. After a year or so, all children were given the injection. If it worked, the San babies would be able to fly and would gain super strength within days. On top of this, they would not require any further care because they could survive almost any type of injury. On the other hand, the human babies, those for whom the injection did not work, were left alone as well. They were left alone so they could die.

By that age, however, more often than not they would not need as much care as a newborn baby, and so some of them would survive.

There were differences between these two. First of all, San babies were given full names, first and last, for the purpose of keeping their family name alive. However, humans had to make up their own names while growing up. Bryan, for example, began calling himself that when he turned five. It was a very popular name and there were at least seven Bryans in the orphanage he grew up in. Also, the Sans would go on to orphanages with facilities that were actually adequate for a baby to grow up in. Even they did not need it, they would get the full protection of the government and a better education as they grew. However, those children who do not show signs of the San abilities were sent to orphanages that were practically farms, simply places for keeping humans, just like the one Bryan had been sent to.

With all their powers, the Sans believed they were good enough to fend for themselves. They did not want to give aid to others nor did they expect help in return. Due to these new morals, the world had changed. First there were no more police to enforce the law. Then, people became more and more selfish, and less caring. The sole reason Sans had jobs was to live more luxuriously. They no longer needed to spend money on food, so their money was spent on entertainment. In this new economy, the best selling products were games, drugs and alcohol. People began to care about each other less and less until the idea of love became obsolete. If there was love, it was secret, and hidden. Through evolution, the new San race lost certain nerves in the brain that allowed them to feel sympathy. However, Bryan was too blinded by his envy for their privileges and powers to notice this.

Soon, even the humans became accustomed to these new ideals and stopped expecting help, trying to give help, nor even having any contact with other humans. Even Bryan isolated himself, or at least tried to. He still felt an urge to talk to people and make friends.

After the fair, before he walked home, he went to talk to the female human he had spotted earlier. He ran to the other side of the street and tried to make conversation.

"Hi, remember me? We met at the specialty store." Bryan said. Once a month, he went to the specialty store to get his monthly food supplies, but every time he came to the store, she seemed to be there. He felt nervous speaking to her as he had not spoken to anyone in a long time. He just stared at the ground, avoiding eye-contact with the girl.

"Oh yeah, I remember, but I can't talk right now, I

don't want to get seen and end up like that guy over there." Bryan's eyes followed the line of her finger as it pointed at the beaten body, and he continued to stare at the ground.

"Okay bye," but the moment Bryan looked up the woman had already gone.

Bryan, having still a lot of things to do could not just head home. He walked through the crowd while one by one they took off to the sky and flew away. Some lived right in the next building while others seemed to leave for a different city.

When everyone else was gone Bryan was still walking down the street. He was the only one walking. The many crowds that filled the streets during the parade were nowhere to be seen and the streets were now empty. There were not many cities left with decent places to walk since the injection came into use, but for the humans, walking was the only way they could get anywhere. In the last few years, Bryan had moved several times looking for a new city, and in every city he moved to, sidewalks were destroyed to make room for more buildings. Each time he moved, Bryan was forced to leave all his belongings because he had to travel by foot.

After many moves from city to city, Bryan had finally decided to stay at this one, Servusville, a city with close to a hundred percent of its population being

Sans. He knew he would be more comfortable in a human town, but he had decided to try blending in with the Sans. He thought by blending in, he would feel less like a misfit or a failure. Although most of the city's populations were Sans, there was a guarantee of permanent sidewalks for humans because the government no longer had enough money to make any more changes.

This also meant that the ground level of the whole city was very dirty and crowded. The center street where the parade had taken place was located in the middle of the city, dividing it into East and West sections. This was the cleanest of all the streets Bryan had ever seen. It was pretty much the only street that was taken care of regularly. The population of the entire world had grown since the injection, until it became so great that the world was no longer big enough to provide wide spaces between each building. The walls of the buildings were so close together that the sidewalks were all that was left of the grounds not occupied with a building. And the little sidewalk space that there was, were often left filled with trash that had been there for months, even for years. City leaders thought it was useless to clean up the mess as it was made by humans and was harmful only to humans themselves, and so they did not waste any tax dollars on maintenance. This responsibility was left for the creators of the filth and grime, but even humans did not care enough to clean it up. Consequently, the piles of trash continued to grow year by year.

The sidewalks seemed to be gray for most of the day due to lack of sunlight. Most of the light was deflected by the surrounding forest of towering skyscrapers, things made of green tinted glass that went on for mile after mile, rising up from the very ground the dark sidewalks were laid out upon. The sidewalks looked like an old black and white film in comparison, and even looked grainy in darkness. However, to the humans, this was normal. They never saw the colorful beauty of the world above them.

Above the ground floors, it was the Sans; kingdom; where there were green painted front doors on every floor of every skyscraper, majestic buildings reaching as high up as 231 stories. Because the population kept growing and there was nowhere else to expand but up, each and every one of these glorious structures "stole" the light from the humans and reflected it back into the surrounding skies.

During the day, the city itself was barely visible because of the blinding light coming from the buildings. And at night, the city was beautiful. The glimmering light from the moon and stars reflected by the buildings, lighting up the city. Individual stars could be distinguished in the glass of the skyscrapers, making small ripples and making each building look like a pond reflecting the sky. The humans, however, could never observe this magnificence.

Bryan looked up as a San suddenly flew over him. As Bryan looked closer he noticed that this San was actually his boss, who was also one of the few who knew of Bryan's being human. Today was a very big holiday and Bryan was allowed to take the day off. He looked enviously at his boss, wishing he could fly as well.

"Hello sir." murmured Bryan. He did not want to be seen talking to a San publicly, even his boss.

Bryan arrived at the specialty store selling food for humans after many nervous minutes of running beneath the shadows of many strange Sans. Although food was not necessary for Sans, San companies had found it profitable to leave food stores for humans.

The store's door was made of glass, although not as pretty as the glass of the Sans. It was covered with stickers advertising all the different kinds of food products offered by San companies.

'Hot dogs! It is the best meat you can find! Buy it or starve!' one poster declared. None of the posters really made Bryan want to buy the product advertised, but he had no other choice.

As Bryan opened the door, he noticed another human walking out, apparently ashamed of his state and staring at the ground. Bryan took one step back and let him pass.

Once he entered, he was overwhelmed by the stench of rotten foods coming from all directions. As he looked around, thinking of what he needed to buy, he noticed the foul smell of rotting vegetables. Bryan thought in regret of how he could be getting better quality food in a human town. However, he also knew that such towns were far too distant for him to walk to. Besides, the only money he had left was the money he had in his pocket now. He had to wait until he received his next salary the following month. Any job given to a human was not going to have a high salary.

Bryan sighed as he thought of the last time he ate food from this store. It was terrible. It made him vomit for three days. Because there was no more need for doctors in the San world, the only ones left were the ones researching a "cure" for humans. So, Bryan had to suffer those three days, knowing there was the possibility of death from malnutrition. This deadly 'so called food' was made with a white blob with a small piece of rotten fish on top of it which was not even cooked. Bryan learned over the years that the best quality in taste came from the food company that was sponsored by the Sans. Because he knew this Bryan once bought everything by this company to find which was the best. That was when he bought the 'death food' by accident. From then on, he avoided it with care. Bryan, quickly but still making sure, grabbed what he needed and headed for the counter.

The cashier was an arrogant adolescent San who believed all humans were too inferior to even be left alive, and had probably only taken the job that involved meeting humans because of its high pay. He was playing his portable game player while Bryan stood patiently, waiting for his food to be checked. The haughty teen looked at Bryan condescendingly and then grabbed at the food that Bryan had picked up.

"One twenty-five ninety-nine" Said the cashier.

"What? "said Bryan, surprised by the extraordinarily high price.

"One hundred twenty-five dollars and ninety-nine cents," the cashier enunciated as if Bryan was too dumb to understand numbers.

"Okay, whatever." Bryan could not argue with a San.

Bryan reached into his pocket. He grabbed all the coins and dollars he had gathered in the morning and struggled to count out the correct amount. The impatient teen sighed in irritation.

"Well, okay. Bag the stuff yourself." The cashier said finally, and turned back to his game.

Bryan did as the cashier said. In the world of the injection, humans were silently known as the lower species and had fewer rights than the Sans. It was understood that humans obviously could not vote nor could they get jobs of the higher class. Further, humans had to go to separate schools from the Sans, where the teachers were often unqualified.

Before he left, Bryan looked around. After he made sure there was no one to notice him coming out of a human store, he ran out and kept running for a few blocks. This was so no one could see his face properly, and was a standard procedure Bryan followed every time he left the store. It was tiring, but being seen shopping for food was one of the worst things that could happen to Bryan.

As he was heading back home, he noticed a poster on the wall. It depicted a handsome man wearing a white band around his head with a green sun symbol on it. That green sun was a symbol of the Sun Worshipers, representing the color of the Sans' skin while the sun represented the Sans' power source. The power source was one of the main things all Sans were proud about. This poster was advertising the parade. It was good that he went to the parade because if he had not, his neighbors would have suspected him of being a human.

Bryan arrived in front of his apartment building. As he looked at the run down sidewalks and the front door of the ground floor, Bryan remembered how he had to specifically ask the landlord for an area where no one else would want to live. There were no more elevators or stair cases any longer, and the only way of getting in any where higher than the first floor was by flying. Because he could not get the first floor without revealing his secret, Bryan had to tell the landlord. The landlord was not a big fan of humans and therefore made Bryan pay full price. So he had to pay the same price for the terrible room as others paid for the prestigious rooms closer to the top.

Bryan entered his house and turned on the light. The light flickered a few times as the old light bulb struggled to burn. He looked around and saw a broken down one-room apartment with various kinds of bugs scrambling around on the floor as the light came on at last. All he had in this room were a bucket, a mirror, a desk, a clock, a phone, a blanket and some makeup.

The dim light made the room look even more depressing. The broken down and ripped apart walls and wallpaper seemed dank and old. Under the remaining wallpaper, little bumps made by bugs moved around quickly, seeking escape. The mirror in the corner was half covered in dust and the bucket contaminated the whole room with its foul odor. The desk, almost never used, was probably the cleanest thing in the room and on it, sat his make up, a blanket and a clock. About six feet from the desk was a window, barely letting any light in. On the windowsill were a plant and a telephone.

It was not very good but it was the best room he'd ever had. It was also the most expensive room he'd ever had. He would have to live off of only a quarter of his salary to pay the rent. Still, the landlord seemed to not like Bryan and it was obvious she was waiting for him to not pay his rent just one time.

Bryan set his meal on the desk and picked a tomato from the plant on his windowsill. He had started growing these tomatoes after getting sick from the sushi at the store. From then on, Bryan tried to avoid anything that seemed even a bit suspicious, including vegetables. He walked over to the table and unwrapped his meal. He remembered as he ate that this would be another start of the short cycle he'd made of the types of food he could eat. Bryan ate in a cycle with a limited variety of foods in a certain order.

However, even after so many meals, Bryan never got used to the taste of this food. He opened another wrapper covering two pieces of bread with some sauce in the middle. This was called a "hotdog." However, to Bryan this tasted the same as "lasagna," "shepherd's pie," and "clam chowder." As he ate his meal, Bryan thought back to his childhood at the human orphanage. He remembered the muddy playground, which was also the children's bathroom, bedroom, and dining room. He especially remembered the long metal bucket he and his "roommates" shared for every meal. Compared to the orphanage meals, Bryan's current fare was amazing.

After his dinner, Bryan ate the tomato he had picked and went to his "bathroom" in the corner to erase his San make up. Bryan had to make a bathroom of his own by putting a bucket and a mirror in the corner. Sans did not have any waste to release because they did not eat. This was one of the reasons sun worshipers worshiped the sun. They did not have any wastes from it.

Although he could not wash his whole body because there were no showers connected in the first floor, he always remembered to wash his make up off. It was too uncomfortable to sleep in.

Bryan cleaned off his makeup by putting his head under the flowing water. Then he dried off all the water with his shirt and went to his sleeping area. He lied down and put his blanket over him. It was a bit early, but he knew he should go to sleep early to wake up ready for his job tomorrow.

Chapter 02

The day after the fair, Bryan had set his alarm clock for 6 o'clock in the morning to get ready for work, but he overslept and almost missed his breakfast. It was important that Bryan eat a lot in the morning because jobs no longer had a lunch break. It took Bryan about 40 to 45 minutes to prepare his extra-large meal and consume it. Then, around seven thirty, Bryan went to his bathroom corner and fixed his San make up for the day. He grabbed his coat and left for his job at an antique shop.

The trip to work took Bryan about thirty minutes, time in which Bryan looked around self-consciously.

As he was walking, Bryan passed the exact spot where the incident had happened yesterday. The man who had gotten beaten up was still lying there. He felt pity for this man. Bryan had even thought of helping him but decided not to. He knew the body would never actually be taken care of, but instead left to rot amidst the garbage of the lower levels

He was still puzzled by the stranger's courageous and stupid act, but was trying to forget it. However, one idea still roamed around in Bryan's head: He should always keep careful to keep his humanity a secret. He did not want to die.

Bryan arrived at work after thirty long minutes. He was exhausted by the time he opened the door to the shop, but what welcomed him was not a nice warm room where he could sleep or rest but the annoying, high pitched voice of his boss.

"Hey, did you go to the parade yesterday? Wait, are humans even allowed?" asked the boss. He chuckled.

His boss was an old San who was nicer than most. This was not because of his particular care for humans but because of his old age, having lost the care and enthusiasm to actively create a line between the two species. However, he still did try to look superior by occasionally making insinuating comments such as: "Bryan, I think you are pretty smart for a human" or

"Bryan, did you steal my money from the cash register?" which he thought to be hilarious.

"Yes sir." Bryan answered, also wanting to tell him about how he'd seen him yesterday but deciding that it was probably unnecessary.

After a long silence while he waited for another one of Mr. Johnson's remarks, Bryan just nodded and went in to get the mop and his gear. The store was just a huge room with many shelves that were filled with useless items. To Bryan, all these items were just blobs of metal that shouldn't even be considered art, but there were often eccentric wealthy collectors that would pay thousands of dollars for such things.

Because of these eccentric people, business was pretty good. There didn't need to be many customers because one item sold would bring a lot of money. With this money, the store was improved. The floor was covered in marble and the walls were all half windows so that people from outside could see all the items there. This shop and the street in front of it was probably one of the cleanest places in all of the first level of the city.

Bryan was the janitor there and he took pride in it. It was not easy for a human to clean such a huge place. Although his original intention was to become a salesperson, his boss thought it was not right for a human to sell something to a San because the customer might feel uncomfortable. The boss thought by being a salesman himself, he would have a bit more time to talk to new people and actually make friends. This was true, so Bryan tried hard to keep from talking to anyone. Bryan knew if he lost this job, he would not be able get another one. At least he had a job while most humans had nothing.

Bryan started mopping the floors. He had to start early so he could finish his work by noon and then, he would be able to just linger until allowed to go home.

"Excuse me." said a feminine voice behind Bryan.

This startled Bryan as he turned around to see who it was. It was a San lady about the same age as Bryan. She was very tall like all Sans and had a smile on her face. She looked at Bryan straight in his eyes, as if she did not care if Bryan was a human or not. In fact, her eyes seemed to brighten, and Bryan looked up cautious of who was seeing the conversation.

This was unusual. Most Sans tried to seem superior by lifting their head and looking down at humans as much as possible. Because of this sudden kindness from a San, it was a bit awkward for Bryan.

"Yes. Uh... May I help you?" he asked.

"Yes. Can you tell me about that item over there? I believe it's called an automobile?"

The automobile was a big red metal object with four leather seats that were grooved in the middle.

Next to one of the seats were a wheel and a handle with letters and numbers next to it. Under the wheel were pedals. The automobile had one door on each side and a big glass wall in the front. On the front hood was drawn a small yellow mark with a horse on it. Under the hood there was another metal object that had many pumps going through it. Also, the automobile was very heavy. It was so heavy in fact, that it even took three Sans to lift it. The only thing the automobile was good for, in Bryan's mind, was that it was a spot where he could occasionally sneak a quick nap without Mr. Johnson noticing.

"Oh, that's an item that hasn't been sold for quite a long time. It's useless though. It's just a big chunk of metal that takes up space. But..." He stopped himself from saying that he slept in it occasionally. The San woman did not seem to notice.

"Really? I think it looks pretty. How much is it?"

"It's... I actually don't know. I'm just a janitor here so, you should ask my boss. I'm sorry."

"Oh, it's fine, so can you tell me where your boss is?"

Bryan looked around, but he could not see his boss anywhere. He was probably watching television again. There was a room behind the shop, which was an employee's lounge that Bryan was not allowed in. Bryan thought it inadequate to call that room an employee's lounge if he himself, the only employee, was not allowed in there. Bryan did occasionally eavesdrop on the sounds from the television set through the door at the end of the store leading to the lounge. However, Bryan's boss spent most of his day there while no one was in his shop. And usually, the shop was empty because no one actually liked to buy things from the past other than rich Sans who had both space in their house and enough money to buy these antiques which were usually very expensive. The automobile was, for example, as Bryan recalled, 120,000 dollars. Bryan had actually already known this but just could not stand talking to the woman any longer.

"Mr. Johnson? Are you there? There's a customer here to ask about the automobile." Bryan called out.

"What? No one buys that thing, but I guess if the customer wants it." answered Mr. Johnson as he reluctantly got up from the couch. "I was watching my favorite show..." he muttered.

"Hello" said the woman as she approached Mr. Johnson.

Knowing the customer was being taken care of, Bryan quietly went back to his business. As he worked, he remembered his childhood. Slowly, he lost focus on his mopping and he fell into his usual daydreams.

It was when Bryan was about seven years old.

Bryan and his friends did not know very much about the world and its classifications of humans and Sans. Because they did not know any better, they believed that they were able to fly, just like the adults. So, one day, Bryan and his friends started jumping off things.

First they started with low things such as the long metal bucket used for eating. They slowly went on to bigger objects. Then they finally went for the biggest of all, the roof of the orphanage.

"You go first," said Bryan as he shoved one of his friends closer to the edge. The house was two stories tall and so they were all scared.

"No, you go," said one friend.

"No, you're the oldest so you should go first." Said Bryan

"Well you're the youngest so you should do what I tell you."

They started fighting. The oldest friend threw the first punch, which Bryan luckily dodged. Then, Bryan punched at his friend. Left, then right, then a left until he had accidentally knocked his friend off the roof. The friend first lost his balance, waving his hands in the air wildly. Then finally, he fell, reaching out for help. Bryan still remembered the look on his friend's face to this day, and some nights had nightmares about it.

The friend had twisted in the air, falling headfirst.

Bryan looked down, seeing a friend he had just been arguing with, a friend who lay there dead with a clearly visible crack on the top of his skull. If he had fallen on his legs, he would have lived...

A friend dying was not new to Bryan, even at that young age. He'd only had about four friends left who were alive at that point, and only three that were actually healthy. Just two weeks previous to the fall, he'd had twelve friends, but seven of them had died because of "small pox."

Due to the lack of proper medical care all the children at the orphanage had to be separated, the healthy from the sick. But, there was not much room in the sty and in the end everyone had the chicken pox. Of those children, Bryan was one of the lucky ones. Luckily, Bryan and two of his friends survived the time they spent in the orphanage and had left just two years ago.

Bryan rubbed his throat. He must be catching a cold again. He had to be extra careful because jobs did not give sick days anymore. Even though Mr. Johnson knew that Bryan was human, he still followed San rules and Bryan could not take the day off for health reasons. The last time he had a cold he was lucky because he had gotten sick on a weekend, so, he did not have to work while he recovered. However, this time, he would have to work even with a cold.

Bryan heard the television set from the employee room as Mr. Johnson turned it on again. The woman had bought the automobile and left the store. Since she was unable to carry it, the item would be mailed to her home.

On the television, there was a rerun of an interview with Mr. Servodeus from three days ago being played again. The interviewer had just asked about Servodeus's opinion on the humans still left powerless today.

"Well, many scientists and I have been working on this problem for years; however, I think we need to have more tests taken on actual humans to know the exact problem. I think if we had a way to get some humans to volunteer for some tests, the new serum would be ready in no time."

"Why can't you just bring in a few human children from the orphanage?"

"We don't want to do anything by force. We want..."

"What are they talking about? Who wouldn't want to become a San?" said Bryan, involuntarily.

"What did you say Bryan? Get back to work!" Shouted Mr. Johnson from the employee lounge.

Bryan quickly ran back to his mops and acted as though he was working. He wandered off in his thoughts again as he remembered when he was thirteen and it was time for his second injection. The scientists had believed that because of the hormonal change from puberty, the genes of the children would change and the injection might work if taken again. This theory had been proven to work only 12 percent of the time but to Bryan, that 12 percent was as good as a guarantee.

Bryan remembered walking into his foster parents' house for the first time to take his second injection. The foster parents were in fact just Sun Worshipers who were placed in the building to make sure the humans got their second injection.

The Sun worshipers did not want to take the risk of losing a perfectly capable San because of the fact that the injection did not work the first time. After the injection, if it did not work, they would throw them back out to the sty, and if they wanted to leave they could and if they wanted to stay they could. At most it just meant less food for the other children.

He'd walked in and gone down the white hallway with tiles everywhere, from the walls to the floor and even the ceiling. This was a luxury that the parents were able to enjoy and Bryan was very happy that soon, he also would be living like this.

He turned right and stepped into another white room filled with lights and people in white suits. He was then strapped down to a blue object that was called a bed. It was shaped like a body of a person with a big thing in the middle with one head sticking out on top and a long thing under the middle one. This soft chair like thing was new to Bryan and it made him even crazier to get the injection so he could become a San, who would be able to use these chairs everyday.

"This will probably hurt, but if it's a success, you will be glad you went through the pain." said one of the people in the white suits. This was also the first time an adult talked to him directly and so kindly. The guards of the orphanage always just stood there and had conversations only between each other. They were just there to make sure nobody escaped. But they would no longer care if Bryan left.

Many painful hours followed the injection, but Bryan endured it thinking of the prestigious life style and so many new privileges he would enjoy if and when he got his powers. He wanted to test them out right after the pain ended but he remembered the doctors telling him that he would have to wait a few days for the abilities to manifest.

Until then, the foster parents allowed Bryan to stay in a warm room of his own while his friends would have to sleep in their own wastes for the night. This was probably because the adults did not know yet if Bryan was going to be a San, and so began treating him like one just to make sure.

They stopped calling him by derogatory human names and no longer looked at him condescendingly. They even called him Bryan, for the first time.

After waiting three long days in a comfortable room with a bed, he finally got to test the injection. The test was, again, jumping off the roof of the orphanage. Bryan knew he would be okay if he flew and even okay if he did not. He had grown up now and would probably not get hurt as long as he landed on his feet. So without any hesitation, he jumped.

At first, he felt as though he was floating a little but he soon realized that he was falling. Simply falling. He landed safely on his feet, which was good news. However, the injection had failed. Once they made sure of the test results, the doctors just left him out there with the rest of his friends as they took another human for the injection. Bryan just kept living in the conditions that had been his before the second injection. He didn't know that he could leave. The foster parents no longer talked nor met Bryan and when they did while filling up the food bucket, they only called him a derogatory term and stared at him.

Even with such a tragic ending, this was one of Bryan's best memories. This was the only time he had ever slept on a bed and ever been treated so nicely. It was heartbreaking though, that he had built up so much excitement and anticipation for such a great and happy life ahead of him, and then all of it had been taken away with just one quick jump.

By noon, Bryan was done. He took his mop and gear and put them in the corner and looked around. He made sure the ground was clean once more and then checked for any customers that he might be able to help. When he didn't see anyone, he decided to just linger around the lounge door and listen to the television set. On it, a news anchor was talking about the parade yesterday.

"The event was spectacular, with..."

Bryan kept on listening for something about the man who had gotten beaten up. However, after about two minutes of talking and a short clip, there was nothing about the man. Slightly disappointed, Bryan stopped listening.

Then the next news report came on. It was about how Mr. Servodeus had requested for financial support from the community to make a camp where humans could be tested and find out why they did not get the abilities enjoyed by the Sans. Bryan was so surprised, words again came out of his mouth involuntarily.

"Mr. Johnson, did you hear that? I might become a San!"

There was no answer. He was probably sleeping.

'He is very old,' thought Bryan, who was ecstatic. This was just like when he turned thirteen and it was time for his second shot.

After about two hours, Bryan had to mop the floors again. Working hard, he wiped the whole ground until it was spotless. This took him about three hours, taking more time as he was still tired from the first run. By the time he was finished, Mr. Johnson seemed to be tired of watching television and got up from the couch. He walked over to the shop and lingered around for a while, obviously not wanting Bryan to leave so early.

After about half an hour or so of doing nothing, Mr. Johnson finally let Bryan leave.

"Bryan, you can go now. It will probably take you about two hours to get home from here, right? I mean, you can't fly so..." said Mr. Johnson as he chuckled under his breath. He probably just wanted to go back to his house and sleep on his comfortable bed, thought Bryan.

Chapter 03

As Bryan left the shop, he looked up. He could not see much but he could make out from the color of light reflected on the higher floors that night was coming. The usually green tinted windows were starting to show glimpses of dark blue and Bryan could barely see five feet in front of him. Suddenly a cold drop of water hit his face and splashed into his eyes. It was raining.

It did not rain much normally, as more and more water consumption was needed for the Sans and humans. The only water that was left in the world was in the sea. Because of this, the wealthiest San companies were in the business of water pumping and purifying, selling it as a product. This was one of the top businesses, along with video games and hydrogen electricity plants. Seeing the rain, Bryan knew he should probably head home faster. He didn't want to get wet.

Bryan started running with his hands above his head, ducking his head in to avoid the water. In this awkward position, he ran for two blocks, passing a few humans who stared at him strangely. The rain soon subsided however, and it was dry once again.

His usual walk to and from work went through the main part of the city where the parade was held. This was the only part of the city where he could actually see the sky. He looked up to see how dark it was, noting that the sky was turning pink and even orange. Then, just out of curiosity, he also checked to see if the body was still here. It was not. Bryan rubbed his eyes and checked again. The body was definitely gone.

'That's weird. I definitely saw him there this morning...'

He kept on pondering on about where the man could have gone. He just stood there for a few moments. Finally, he concluded that the man had not actually been dead, and had crawled away somewhere. Deciding to leave as well, Bryan found he could not.

A bunch of sun worshipers were walking in front of

him. Bryan had been so distracted by his thoughts that he had not seen these men coming his way. He was petrified now. They were obviously high or drunk and there were five of them. All of them were young adults and were wearing the same green shirt and headband as the ones he'd seen yesterday. Bryan tried to act calm and hoped that they were just walking and/or too drunk to notice him.

'This is the main part of the city and it is the widest street. Maybe they're just coming here to take off as a group, or maybe this is the way to their homes....' A rush of thoughts entered and left his mind as he just stood there, terrified, and anxiously wishing they would not come near him. Just wishing they would go somewhere else or fly away.

Then, his wishes were crushed with a sudden break of words.

"Look at that crap head. Hey, how does it feel to live in the same place as your crap?" said one of them. He was not even pronouncing the words correctly because he was too drunk. However, this must have been a funny joke or something because the whole group started laughing hysterically. Bryan could guess why these guys were laughing. He tried to laugh with them to break the ice, but he couldn't.

The Sun Worshipers liked to call humans names having anything to do with the wastes that humans have to release. They thought that humans were disgusting and low creatures that lived in a cage where they slept, defecating and eating all at the same place. This was correct in some ways, because those descriptions were pretty much how human orphanages were organized.

"Excuse me. I'm just going to my house," murmured Bryan. He was staring at the ground. He had nowhere to go. The streets were too narrow and even if he had somewhere to go he would never be able to outrun a San, never mind five of them.

"You have a house? I thought you lived in the streets. How do you even afford a house?" The sun worshiper said.

Bryan did not answer and just kept staring at the ground. He knew he was going to get beaten up no matter what, but he did not want to make it worse by saying anything that might make the group even more aggressive. He also believed deep down that he could avoid this by just being quiet and taking all the hate-filled comments. He wished badly to be a San at that moment. If he were a San, he would not even have to be in this mess. Even if he was, he could just fly away.

"Hey, I asked you a question..." the sun worshiper said, continuing to blab on about how Bryan was so dirty, low and poor. Bryan just decided not to listen, looking for his chance.

And there it was. Bryan saw that these Sun Worshipers were definitely drunk and were too carried away by their own constant spiel of not particularly funny jokes. Bryan tried to quietly sneak past them as they laughed. It was a big risk, but he was willing to take it in order to get out of this mess.

The first step was taken, and Bryan turned to see if anyone noticed. No one. Good, now the second step...

"Hey where do you think you're going? What, do you have to go crap in your house?" One of them said. Everyone started laughing again. Bryan knew now, he had nowhere else to go.

The first San grabbed Bryan by his clothes and pushed him into another San. They started laughing as they played a sick ball game with Bryan being the ball.

Then, they pushed Bryan to the ground and started beating him. One kick here and one kick there. After the first two kicks, he wanted to faint and lose consciousness. He did not want to feel all this suffering. However, each time he thought he could escape in that manner, he was instead woken up even more from the pain.

It worked its way all over his body. From his head to his toe, his whole body was now hurting. He had been through fights with other humans before in the orphanage, but they were nothing like this. The fight for the jump for example, was nothing. The other kid had been older than him and yet, Bryan was able to beat him. Now that he thought of the fights in the orphanage, the pain then was less than a tickling. This was real pain. This was even more than his sicknesses and all his near death experiences. This was a thousand times, no a million times more painful. This experience made Bryan realize again, how Sans were far more powerful and superior to him.

Bryan wished he were a San. If he were a San, he would not even be in this mess. If he were a San, he would at least be able to fight back and have a small chance. If he were a San, he would be able to heal from this and he would not feel so much pain. If he were a San...

The beating went on until one of the Sun Worshipers got bored.

"He's dead. Lets go," and they all flew away.

They didn't have to deal with any law or another San telling them what to do. Laws still existed, but no one had to abide by them because there were no police. Without police, the Sun Worshipers were the monarchy of the new world. They were the ones in charge. Bryan was just another toy that they could play with. He didn't have any help coming. Strangely, even though he knew this, he kept waiting and waiting...

As Bryan was going though this immense amount

of pain, time around him slowed down. Bryan saw the Sans fly away. He noticed the sun was falling. The diminishing sunlight glittered against the green glass above him and created a spectacular show of bright light. It was getting darker and Bryan knew the beauty would only last so long. Soon, it would be night, and he would no longer be able to find himself home. He wanted to get up. He had to.

The beating had lasted for less than ten minutes, but for Bryan, it had been an eternity. All over his body, it felt as though the beating was still happening. He wanted it to stop, but it wouldn't. He wanted to get up and walk back home, but he couldn't. His home was only 5 minutes of walking from here, he thought. If only his body would listen to him. Bryan longed for at least his arms to work, so he could slap himself across the face and say to himself, "Suck it up."

But there was only himself to blame.

'If I didn't get out of work so early, I wouldn't be here. If I didn't run when the rain came, I might have missed those Sun Worshipers. If I didn't stand there just thinking like an idiot, I might have been out of this street when the Sans came along...' Bryan could have gone on with an infinite list of what could have happened instead of what did happen, but he had to stop himself; Bryan had to go back to his house.

But there was an invisible force fighting against

him. Bryan kept trying to get up and fight against the force making him want to close his eyes. He didn't want to die. He was too young. He hadn't even lived a proper life yet.

Then he thought again.

'I don't have a life to live. I made those choices and if I was a San, I would be able to recover from this right away, but I can't. It is my fault entirely. If I die now, I might be doing the rest of the world and even myself a favor. Maybe my next life will be better than this. Maybe my next life, I could be a San...'

Bryan then accepted that it was his turn to die, just like the man from the parade. He closed his eyes and held his breath. If the beating did not do the job, then suffocation would finish it. He wanted to do anything to quicken this death so he would not hurt any more. But suddenly, though it might have been a dream, he heard a voice.

"Where do you live?"

Bryan told this anonymous person where he lived and tried to die again. Then, Bryan felt as though he was being lifted up in the air and carried. He wondered if this was what it felt like to die. But suddenly he felt a familiar blanket covering him. Bryan opened his eyes and first noticed a floating thing next to him. He then looked around. He saw his familiar desk, phone, bucket, mirror and then the floating thing again.

It was floating? Bryan opened his eyes again and observed this thing.

"It" was actually the San that had been at the antique shop. Bryan remembered her asking for the expensive automobile.

'What is she doing here? Why would a San...' Bryan dozed off into a deep sleep as the San poked something into his arm.

When Bryan woke up, he noticed something different about his house. A nice bed replaced his blankets on the floor, even better than the one he had once slept on in the orphanage. His table was replaced by nice mahogany furniture decorated with a sheet and an antique item on top of it. His little corner of a bathroom was gone and was replaced by a nice closet. Bryan could not believe his eyes. He had to check this out.

When he tried to get up expecting to fall over, he got up with ease instead. So easy in fact, that he felt as though the beating had never even happened. His body felt lighter than he remembered. He lifted up his right foot. He wiggled it around in the air. He could not feel anything. After he checked all of his limbs thoroughly, he wanted to make sure he could walk, but first, he would have to see if his legs were strong enough to withstand even a jump. He was hesitant because maybe when he lands, the force will over pressure the already fractured legs and end up breaking them. But in the end, he decided, what the hell, given the fact that just being able to walk was a miracle anyways. He did not have much to lose if he broke his legs.

"Okay, One, Two, Three." Bryan closed his eyes and jumped.

He waited and waited but he could not feel anything under his feet. He didn't feel the thump under his feet from falling. He wiggled his foot around in the air, trying to catch some sort of hard surface. But the only hard flat surface he could grasp was too far away to be the ground. He opened his eyes to see what was happening.

Like he had expected, when Bryan looked down, he saw the floor. However, he observed that the floor was further away from him than it usually was. On top of this, he couldn't feel the floorboards beneath his feet.

'What's happening? Did I grow?' Bryan was confused until he looked at his feet, both hovering in the air, a good foot above the floor of his apartment.

"I'm floating!" Bryan shouted. He couldn't control himself. This was the happiest moment of his life. He was so happy in fact, he even forgot about considering the question of how this was happening.

He flew over to the door. He wanted to fly everywhere he could, before he lost it. First, he wanted to fly around the city and explore what the city was like above the lower floors. He opened the door and flung himself out. To his amazement, he was already well above the first story. He was in fact somewhere above many of the other surrounding buildings. He was flying in the mainstream of Servusville and he could see hundreds of people flying around him.

Bryan could not believe his eyes. The world was so beautiful, so bright and so clean, just like he had hoped it to be. He could not believe he had been living, not even knowing a world like this existed.

A San passed by him and glanced over at him.

'Oh no! My make up!' he looked at his arms. Again, he was amazed by what he saw. His usually bony, bright skinned arms and dark arm hair were gone, his expectations instead met with a muscular green limb with bristly green hair covering it. He looked at his hands and down at his legs; his whole body had become bright green. He had become a San.

Again, he was so filled with bliss at the discovery that he forgot the question of how, and simply flew off into the soaring crowds of Sans. He greeted everyone around him with a great big smile and a loud "hello." Of course no one replied but he didn't care. He was a San.

He flew around among these Sans not even being noticed, let alone being stared at condescendingly. This was the happiest moment of his life. And for once, he actually had a life. After a few minutes of flying among the green tinted skyscrapers, he went to the street where he had been beaten up. He didn't want to land because he thought, 'if I land, I might never be able to fly again.' So, he simply floated above this large open street that held so many memories. He just floated there thinking back to the parade and how the beaten man had disappeared. After this silent moment of meditation, He flew away.

That was when everything went wrong. He felt a cool shiver go down his back. He could feel the usual suspicion and attention from all the crowds around him. He didn't want this feeling coming back to him again. He didn't want the voices next to him saying, 'Look at him, he's so dirty, He's like a monkey. No, he's worse than a monkey.' These statements made him actually feel less than a monkey. He had never even seen an actual monkey, but he knew it was used as a derogative term. He was mourning his misfortunes when a thought struck him.

'Maybe my make up is wearing off!'

Bryan looked down at his body, discovering that it was slowly returning to its normal state. The greenish color was fading away and his normally tan features were coming back. He felt embarrassed again. He wished he had just stayed home so he could save himself all this attention.

He tried to fly away, but he couldn't. He was no longer flying and was stuck there standing in the middle of the street. Then, one by one people started to gather around him. These people began saying bad things about him and soon enough, there was a full chorus of people mocking him and attacking him mercilessly. Among these people, even human friends whom he'd met in the orphanage were there. Bryan felt as though he was the only human in the world, as if he was stuck in a zoo cage to be seen and poked at.

"Stop!" Bryan cried out, starting to run. He ran and ran but he was going nowhere. No matter how fast he tried to run away, he was still among the throng. However, after a long time of sprinting, he at last made it out of the crowd and ran over to the nearest street. There, he ran over to the antique shop. Before he entered, he looked above him. All the buildings were gone and a huge shadow filled the space, which used to contain the buildings. This shadow was a huge group of flying Sans with the sole intention of following Bryan. They were like demons following him for his soul. This was an inescapable nightmare.

Bryan quickly opened the door and entered the shop. However, the first step he took he fell into an abyss. He fell and fell and everything that had surrounded him faded into a huge and empty black hole. He could no longer tell if his eyes were open or if he was even thinking or speaking. He was trapped in a huge snare of opaque nothingness.

Thump. He felt the sharp pain and vibration traveling up from his feet and spreading all around his legs from the long drop. He fell over without having the strength to withstand the weight of his own body, a weight multiplied with the drop and thrown against him in impact. After a long moment, Bryan brushed his legs and sat up, but he could still see nothing. Still, he was trapped in this black hole, though he seemed to be set atop some type of solid surface. He got up at last and started to walk around.

'At least I am standing. Maybe this is a good thing. No one is going to judge me here.'

Just then, he could see a faint light coming from the distance. It seemed like the crack of a door ajar. From the crack, he heard children fighting. The sound of the children's voices got louder with each step he took towards the door. He ran over and when he reached this faint light, he could see it was in fact a closed door with light coming from beneath it. The sound of the children's argument was now turned into a brawl of screams and crying. He opened the door and entered.

Once he entered he was standing in a small muddy cage with a pile of dead bodies on one side. On the other side, there was a building and next to the building was a huge metal slop bucket. Bryan immediately recognized this as his old orphanage. He looked around to see where all the children were. No matter where he looked, there was nothing but open space and corpses. A chill climbed up his back when he looked at the dead bodies. The corpse were all facing towards him and seemed to have a grin on their faces, with their eyes just staring at him.

He followed the screams and looked up towards the top of the building. He could see two children arguing there. Behind the two children there was a group of kids that did nothing to stop the two from fighting. Even they seemed to not pay any attention to the danger the children were in, but instead only stared at him, their mouths held in stiff grins. The clash of the two emotions placed on each face made Bryan scared. So scared, he almost missed what the two arguing children were even talking about.

"You go first," said one of them as he shoved the other closer to the edge. Bryan could make out that the two were both scared of doing something.

"No, you go," said the friend.

"No, you're the oldest so you should go first." Said the other.

"Well, you're the youngest so you should do what I tell you."

They started fighting. Although one was older, they were both roughly about the same size due to malnutrition. A punch was thrown, which the younger child luckily dodged. Then, a punch was returned, setting off a series of blows between the two. Left, then right, then a left until one was accidentally thrown from the rooftop. He fell headfirst. If he had fallen differently, he would have probably just broken his legs. However, he fell headfirst onto the metal feeding bucket.

Bryan quickly ran over to the boy to see if he was alive. When he got there, the child's eyes were closed and there was no sign of life.

"Kid, are you okay?" Bryan asked anxiously. He shook the body rapidly. Bryan had seen too many deaths, and he didn't want to see another one. Especially he didn't want to see two deaths happen here, at the same place. The kid suddenly opened his eyes.

"You! Why did you push me off? You little...." The kid died with his eyes still open.

Bryan pushed the eyes closed and looked up. He could faintly see the other kid looking down at him and the body. He tried hard to make out the face.

"Who is that?" Bryan shouted as he looked carefully at the boy on the roof. He could see a child closely resembling himself.

Bryan rubbed his eyes and opened them again. However, when he opened his eyes, he was no longer in the orphanage. He looked around and could see that he was once again on the main street of Servusville again.

'Oh, maybe that was all in my head,' Bryan thought, 'But to make sure...'

He looked up to see if any one was following him like before. Luckily, no one was.

Just then, he heard a bunch of voices laughing hysterically. When he looked over, he could see five people surrounding another, and all were talking and laughing. Then as he looked closer, he could tell that they were actually five Sun Worshipers surrounding a human.

"You have a house? I thought you lived in the streets. How do you even afford a house?" The five surrounding people started to laugh again.

Bryan had a small longing to help that person. He knew what it felt like to be in that situation. It had just happened to him a day ago. However, he just could not gather up the courage to do so. So, he just kept on watching, rather than do anything.

After a couple more comments, the Sun Worshipers started hitting the surrounded human. This beating went on for about ten minutes or so. During this period of time, Bryan had to stop himself several times from going to help the person. Each time he stopped himself with the same words:

"You can't do anything even if you want to help." Each time, Bryan was stopped instantly when he thought of these words.

However, he desperately wanted to help that person, simply because he had been in the same situation before and knew how he himself had wanted help. And so he waited until the Sun Worshipers were gone so that he could go over to the person on the ground.

Reaching the person, Bryan asked, " Are you okay?" He looked down. Lying there bleeding was Bryan himself, and he was trying to gather the strength to keep from dying. This replica laid there talking to himself.

"Don't die. You didn't have a proper life yet."

"No, You don't...." Bryan slapped his lying replica in the face in order to stop himself from thinking what he himself had thought of before.

This replica looked up at him with wide eyes and soon, all the cuts and bruises were disappearing. Then, his face morphed into a bright green one with the features on the face slowly changing as well. This replica, whom used to be Bryan, was turning into one of the Sans that had hit Bryan.

The San pushed Bryan off from on top of him and

got up. Bryan stumbled back in surprise and tired to run away. However, once again, he couldn't. He was running and running but he was going nowhere. He looked back wishing for this San to have left, but he was still there. In fact, this San was duplicating itself, increasing in numbers one by one. Soon there were hundreds of Sun Worshipers surrounding Bryan. Then all at once, they jumped at him...

Bryan twitched his leg and the sharp stinging pain woke him. He opened his eyes and looked down at his body. It was just like he had dreamed. He then tried to get up but as he tried, his chest and everything in his body started hurting again.

Chapter 04

N1E2

Bryan struggled to turn his head, and looked over at his clock. The red glowing light he could always count on for the time showed him something entirely out of the blue. It said 11:45 A.M. He knew this was not true. He needed it to not be true. There should have been an alarm that went off. Or did he sleep through it. All these thoughts were overruled by one giant worry.

'What about work?'

He couldn't go to work but he knew he should. He didn't want to get fired. It was a miracle that he even had a job.

He looked down at his body. It was covered

almost entirely with comfortable white bands that were better than his blankets. Yet they seemed more like an impediment now since they strapped him so tightly he could barely move. Maybe that was a good thing, but these things were so very new to him. He had never encountered them before. Although the straps limited his body, he gathered from the experience when he tried to get up that restraint from movement kept his body from hurting too much. Also, the coverings kept him warm. However all this was irrelevant right now for his job was on the verge of being lost.

Bryan looked over at his clock again, and knew that now was around the time he would normally be done cleaning the floors for the first time. He hoped Mr. Johnson was asleep in the employee lounge like he always was, not noticing Bryan's absence. He yearned for it to be true.

He was angry with his own body. He wanted to move, but the tight wrappers restricted him. On top of this, whenever he flexed his muscles trying to loosen the straps, his whole body radiated with pain and he involuntarily screamed in both agony and frustration. Why does his body hurt so much, even with the blankets that are holding him in place?

'Okay, let my body hurt. But why can't I even move? These stupid things are too tight.'

At that moment, only two things were clear in his

mind and they both pertained to his standing up or at least gaining some type of motion. The first was that he had to go to work. The second was of less importance. It was that even if he didn't go to work, there were many other things that required his standing up. He had to get up to eat. He had to get up to use the bathroom. Further, his throat was parched and the lack of water seemed to affect his body entirely. First were his lips. His chapped lips began to crack and he could taste blood in his mouth. He could go on and on, in the same way he could make a list of how much better his life could be if he were a San.

Bryan rambled on about all the pessimistic things concerning his situation at that moment, knowing deep down that this would not change anything. Nevertheless, he kept doing it because, although it would not help situation one bit, he could at least get some sympathy from himself, being the only person there. For Bryan, receiving sympathy or pity was a good thing because it meant there was someone who cared about him even if that someone was only himself. It was just another way of consoling himself when it came to the misfortunes of his life.

Bryan soon got tired of this self-comforting and was ready to actually try to fix things. He soon realized though, that he couldn't do anything. So, having nothing else to do, Bryan leaned back and stared at the ceiling when he noticed a sign or some type of message written on it.

'Was that always there? I've never noticed it.' Bryan knew instantly after he thought this that he must have been too busy pitying himself.

WILL BE BETTER IN A DAY OR TWO. DO NOT MOVE.

Bryan, using his weak reading skills, sounded it out as best he could. "W...will be...be...t...t...ter i...in a da...ay... o...r... two. D...do n...ot m...o...ve."

These words were written in red and it was definitely new. They were also the most beautifully written words he had ever seen.

Bryan had learned how to read in the orphanage. However, he had never seen such beautiful handwriting before. Each letter was like a painting with a dynamic and a unique touch applied to it. The best part was that it was still actually legible.

The teachers in the orphanage had written in a way that was barely legible. Consequently, Bryan thought that was how it was usually written and that the only way words could be legible was when they were printed out, like on the posters. Yet, on Bryan's ceiling, there was a beautiful sentence of 11 words written in the most impressive handwriting he had ever seen, contradicting everything he had learned and believed as a reader.

Due to the words' extreme beauty, all Bryan's past opinions of handwriting were quashed. The words seemed to have an overwhelming force that radiated from them. It was almost as if anything written so beautifully must be followed. Bryan decided to do as it said

Following the instructions, Bryan just laid there doing nothing, and tried to forget any worries concerning work. It was hard at first because work took up most of his mindset these days; however, once he got the hang of it, it was easier. In fact, forgetting about work made him much happier and even made it seem that his body hurt less.

'This is better than I thought,' He mused.

Bryan was ready to lie there for hours and hours and maybe take a nap or two. In fact, he was looking forward to the best few hours of his long pathetic life. To start things off, he decided to take a short little nap.

Just then, just when he was about close his eyes and fall asleep, his phone rang. Obviously, he couldn't get it because he could not move. Nor did he want to because the sign told him not to.

'Who would be calling me? Why do I even have a phone? That's such a waste of money that I could be spending on food.' He thought. The humor in the idea brought him a slightly better mood. Although the drugs he had been given had worn off long ago, the numbness of his mind still was present and he was not thinking straight. He knew he was temporarily forgetting something that should be taking up most of his mind.

Unfortunately, he was then reminded of the workday. Everything he had strived for all morning, trying to forget and relax, was ruined. Again, he was hit with a rush of concerns, most of which he had thought through already.

'What if it's Mr. Johnson? What if he's calling to fire me? Then I won't have a job and I can't pay my bills. Then I might get kicked out of this house because I can't pay off the debt....'

The torrent of thoughts rushing into his head refused to stop. It was like being attacked by an invincible monster made of infinite amounts of dark ideas. And soon, two new monsters joined in, except this time, they were fighting against each other.

Not surprisingly, Bryan went in a little panic attack again, the new monsters of fear and curiosity fighting inside him at the same moment as the monster of dark thoughts was attacking him. The monster of curiosity pressed the attack voraciously, and although Bryan did not want to get the phone, he still wanted to know who was calling him. The monster of fear was stealing from the monster of pessimism and using them both as his counter attack. This battle was never ending, and Bryan knew that the only way in which this melee inside of him would cease was for the phone to stop ringing.

So, he waited and waited. The ringing of the phone stung his ear as Bryan twisted and turned in agony. He wanted the ringing to cease or at least for it to go to a message. He waited thirty seconds. Then forty then...

His wish soon came true.

'That was close, maybe it was a wrong number,' he thought in relief.

Bryan now knew that he could spend the rest of the day doing what he had planned to do before. He looked over at the clock, and was relieved by the fact that there was a whole day waiting. The clock said 12:15, its bright red light managing to brighten the room a bit, giving it a/very relaxing atmosphere.

Bryan decided to take a little nap. Unfortunately, he was met with something unexpected as he dozed. Apparently, the day was not going to be as enjoyable as planned, for he soon enough dreamt the same nightmare he had had yesterday.

Another large ringing sound waked him up. When he woke up and looked over, still a little sleepy, he still couldn't figure out what the sound was. He could have sworn he heard the same noise he'd heard when the swarm of Sans had been pursuing him. He soon found out that the ringing noise was coming once again from his phone.

Once again the monsters of fear and curiosity were carried along by the monster of pessimism, and now the lot of them were having a fracas. However, this time the monsters did not last very long, and Bryan soon decided that the phone was going to stop ringing as it had before.

He was wrong however, and the phone kept ringing for what felt like hours to Bryan. No matter how hard he tried to block out the noise and the rest of the world like he had before, he couldn't. Nor could he take a nap to make time fly because of the sound.

He looked over at the clock. It said 2:25. The comforting red light he longed so much to work its magic did not do much this time. The red light simply turned and showed another face. It seemed to be laughing at him.

This was about the time when he should be cleaning the floors again, and also the time when Mr. Johnson would get bored of staying in the lounge. Usually, this boredom resulted in efforts to make Bryan work harder. Since Bryan was not there today, there would be nothing to satisfy Mr. Johnson's boredom. This was just another reason for the phone call to be from his boss.

Bryan banged his head against the phone in

frustration despite the pain that shot all throughout his body. His fingers twitched in agony as he screamed and banged his head.

Just then, the phone stopped ringing and a message started to play automatically.

"Bryan, this is your boss. You are lucky I am such a nice person because you would be fired in an instant anywhere else. A human missing work! That is unacceptable! If you miss one more day, I will, not might, I will fire you. If you think I am joking, you are wrong! You know what? I think I will have to take this out of your salary!"

Bryan was so shocked by this message, that even with the pain, his body went numb. He felt as though he was separated from his body and he was looking at himself from above. He could just picture it, the face and body of a pathetic, crippled human who would soon be dead without any way of rising again; he couldn't even think properly.

'I can't get fired. But I can't get up. But what if I can't leave tomorrow? I won't be able to eat or keep this house. If I don't have a house, I will have to live outside. If I live outside, I will get beaten up all the time. Maybe even more than yesterday.'

These thoughts were passing through his mind but deep down he knew this was no use. All he could do now was just wait to lose his job, able to do nothing about it. He swung his fist against the floor in frustration, but the pain was nothing compared to the thought of himself dying when he could have avoided it by walking six feet.

Even though he knew it was useless, however, he couldn't lose the sensation of sorrow inside of him. It was so hard to get this job. In fact, it was one of his most prized achievements. He didn't have many achievements to remember. This one however, he could remember it like it was yesterday.

It was about a year ago when he had decided to move to Servusville. He did not know how he was going to live. However, he had a volition that he would live in this city and he would no longer move. He was too tired and he didn't have enough money to buy a new place.

First, he looked for a house he could rent. He went around the city and looked at posters and signs for cheap apartments. He was surprised to see that this was fairly easy. He found a pretty cheap room where he could persuade the landlord that he had to live on the first floor. He said he would get it and moved in.

He was able to find the place where he could live, but he could not find any money. He was asked, more like demanded, to pay the first rent within three days. Bryan had expected this when he was moving and so he had saved up his money. He had reached into his pockets and paid all he had.

However, he had miscalculated and had saved up only enough money for the first month's rent. After he paid the landlord, he had no more money left. He would have to find a job or else he would starve to death. So, with that problem in his hands, he looked around the town for shops that he could work at, shops situated along the lower levels of the city. First, being human, he went to the human specialty food store.

He went in and went straight to the counter to ask for a job. For some reason, he was overly confident. Maybe it was the thrill of getting a new job in a new city or maybe it was because he had slept in a new apartment even bigger than his last. Anyways, he was confident.

The cashier was a teenage San and was half asleep. He was definitely bored from working in an empty shop all day. His red hair was all greasy and his braces were bulging from his mouth as his lower lip hung out with drool slipping down. Now that Bryan thought back, all the cashiers in that shop looked bored all the time.

"Excuse me, could I get a job here?" Bryan asked politely. He was yet to know the ways of talking to a San. He was only out of the orphanage about six months and he had moved too many times to actually learn of the real life outside of the orphanage.

All he knew was that there were bad Sans out there willing to hurt you. What he did not know was that all Sans had some pride in them and wanted them to be seen to be better than humans.

He was yet to learn the most important rule of the San world: Do not talk to a San if you are a human, unless it's a matter of life or death. Even then you probably wouldn't get a great response.

This question was obviously not as intriguing to the cashier as it was to Bryan and was rejected immediately.

"No. Get out if you are not buying anything." said the cashier. Bryan's confidence did not pay off after all.

Now that Bryan thought back on this subject, he could understand that the cashier was probably not the owner and that he had asked the wrong person the wrong question.

However, this was also the best thing that happened to him because he immediately learned from that experience that he should make sure to be much more courteous when talking to a person, more importantly to a San. These short "interviews" with the Sans and shop owners of the first few places he went to were where Bryan learned most of his survival techniques in living in a non-human town.

Bryan, keeping these tactics in mind, went around to a few more places. Each interview-slash-rejection gave him more and more experience that he could use in the next. Despite his six months out of the orphanage, it was those couple of days that taught him the most on how to live in the real world instead of the little enclosures he was so used to.

This cycle went on for the following two days. On the last day, he was no longer confident and was ready to admit defeat. He was practically giving up and so he decided to console himself. He could feel his stinging hunger churn inside of him. He knew that he could probably last a day if not less without food.

"One last shop and if you don't get it, well, you don't have any other choice but to starve. It's probably going to end up in you dying." Bryan told himself. This was more like a threat than anything comforting, really.

He walked over to the antique shop, which was the cleanest of the shops along the first level of the city, even back then. He had left this shop for last because first of all, he did not like the idea of working in an antique shop. He had never even heard of antiques before. On top of that, the whole atmosphere of the shop did not seem too inviting. The area itself was quite clean; however, everything else about it did not seem as new or unspoiled. The sign was half broken and only the 'a' and 't' lit up with light. Merely looking at the sign made Bryan regret the fact he had even walked toward the shop. Second of all, he thought he would not fit in on such a clean looking part of the street. He considered himself too dirty, too low. He just did not think he would fit in.

Before he entered the store, he took a deep breath. Again, he spoke to himself, except in a more positive way this time.

'Okay, last chance. You can do this. You have had plenty of practice. Even if you don't like this job, it's the only way. Also, you might turn out to like it.' Although he knew it to be true, he did not want to include the fact that he likely could not get the job at all in his pep talk.

He walked in expecting maybe a little group of objects here and there and was totally bewildered by what he saw. He was absolutely wrong. The whole room was filled with shelves and shelves of items, most of them being things he had never even seen before. Right as he entered the store, he changed his mind about not wanting to work here. He knew that made him a hypocrite, but the room was just so convincing. This was the best job he could ask for. He wanted this job, badly.

With the only thought in his mind being that he wanted the job, he walked straight to the counter and rang the bell. A fairly old San came out of the back room, seeming to be a bit sleepy.

"Yes?" the old man said, rubbing his eyes a moment before his facial expression changed immediately. "You're not a San, what are you doing here?" he asked. Apparently, the man was able to distinguish a San from a human very well because Bryan had been wearing his make up then. Usually, the bosses did not know until he told them, often reluctantly.

"Uh...." Bryan could not get any words out of his mouth. Unlike before, he had actually wanted this job and was nervous. He was also pressured by the fact that he had to get the job or he would probably starve to death.

"Get on with it. What are you doing here?" the old San had said, getting annoyed.

Bryan had to say something or else he knew he was going to get kicked out. So, quickly, he said the first thing in his mind.

"I need a job here or else I will starve. So please can I get a job? I would prefer a selling job but I am willing to do anything as long as it pays," Bryan blurted out.

"A job? Starve? A human?" Mr. Johnson was flabbergasted by all this new information coming at him at once.

"First of all, why does a human need a job? Never mind that. Why do you think you should get a job while other humans out there don't?" Mr. Johnson asked.

"Well...uh.... I don.t know about the other humans but... please sir. I haven't eaten anything in two days." Bryan replied. Bryan could remember his eyes watering as Mr. Johnson laughed in his face in response, as if wanting to show off that Sans did not need food.

"No." Mr. Johnson had said at last. "Actually, I don't know. Come back later, but the answer will still be no. However, I can think of a better deal. If you promise to never come back to this store, I will give you money right now."

Then, there was nothing in Bryan's head but the fact that he needed money for food. So, Bryan gladly took the money and ran straight to the human specialty store to buy a "hot dog". As he paid the cashier, he opened the wrapper and shoved the whole thing into his mouth in one quick motion.

He had tried other foods from other towns before but that hot dog was the best food he had ever eaten. Now that Bryan thought back on this, he couldn't understand why it never tasted the same again. He had tried the same method many times after, but what he always ended up with was not the same glorious delicacy but rather a painful stomachache that sent him scrambling to his corner bucket every few minutes.

That money was enough to last Bryan a few days however, but Bryan had known he would have to get more money sooner or later. Five dollars would only last him a few days especially since he'd been starving for a while already. He knew he would run out soon. When he had lived in the human town before, he was able to get a job so much easier. He was beginning to regret his move. Well, it hadn't been his choice really, because the city had been demolished to make more room for Sans.

As he'd sat outside the specialty store eating his hot dog, he knew if he wanted the job at the antique store, he would have to go back again. He did have a few more shops he had crossed off in the beginning because he thought they were far too distant from his house, but all he had in his mind now was the antique shop and only that. He did not want any other job and he would do whatever it would take to get it. However, the old man had told him not to come back to the shop. That would be a major setback in his goal.

"Maybe it is a test to see my dedication? Or what if he takes away the money he already gave me for coming back? What am I going to do then? I'll be right back where I started. Maybe I'll be heading towards death again,"

He didn't know what to do. He knew there was no way for him to give back money he had already half spent. But that wasn't even half the problem; Bryan knew Mr. Johnson, being a San, was more than capable of taking away what he gave to Bryan, or even more.

Having only been out in the real world for a couple years, all Bryan could do was try to find something to blame for his problems or try to think that they hadn't really happened, but deep down, even with all those thoughts, he knew he had a problem and he would have to deal with it. When Bryan returned to his house, he looked in the mirror. Through the reflection, he could see a stupid looking human, covered in fake green makeup that contrasted with the red light coming from the clock. Even to himself, Bryan looked pathetic. Bryan, having nothing to eat in his house, went straight to bed. He wanted to fall asleep but his mind was so filled with the stress of what lay ahead, that he could barely close his eyes for more than a few seconds.

After a restless night, he decided to go to the shopowner and be content with what ever he said. He was already in the worst possible situation, and he was able to take it. He knew, whether he tried or not, that the worst that could happen would be his death, and so he would rather die trying than sitting there waiting to starve to death.

He walked over to the store for the first fifteen minutes or so with nothing in his mind. He was too anxious and expecting the worst to be thinking overly much or doing any of his usual introvert activities in his head. Then, as he got closer he could feel himself growing more and more tense. He was afraid. Even though he knew exactly what would happen, his human instincts made him have the slightest glimpse of hope, a hope that made him even more anxious and nervous. In what felt like a second, he was already standing in front of the store door.

Again, he steadied himself into not being nervous, took a deep breath and reached for the door when suddenly, the door opened by itself. He staggered from his own forward motion meeting nothing but air but when he gained his balance again and looked up, he saw not what he was expecting.

Mr. Johnson was smiling in a haughty yet kind manner. Bryan, confused, got up straight and stared at him. He could not look away.

"I guess you really do need a job," Mr. Johnson said. "I will just have to take the money I gave you out of your salary."

Bryan, still astonished, nodded dully and quickly added a fake laugh or two as Mr. Johnson kept blabbering on about on how he would never get sick days or free days unless he tells him, but to Bryan's ears, only one thing was taken in properly.

"I'll give you a job..." was what he heard, and all the rest was a blur.

Ever since that moment, Bryan had a bond with Mr. Johnson; however, that moment was the nicest his boss had ever been. Since then, although he was the nicest San Bryan had ever met, he was still not the friendliest person in the world.

Chapter 05

When Bryan woke up, it was dark in the room. Although, this was not the only thing he noticed that was different. The constant pressure of the linen strips covering his body had loosened up and he was able to move his arms again. Miraculously, his arms were not hurting either.

This was lucky because he was starving. He hadn't noticed all this before, but now, he was beginning to feel his stomach churn. After all, the last time he had eaten was two days ago before he left for work. He had gone much longer without eating before, but this time his body actually needed more nutrients because of his injuries.

Without thinking, he did the worst thing he could do to his whole body. Pain and all, he just headed for the nearest food package. His stomach's painful grasping for food was too overpowering for him to care about the rest of his body. The distance from his blankets to his kitchen table however, never felt so far before. He climbed the floor like a ladder thinking he was getting closer, but when he looked up the table would still be too far to reach by hand.

Consequently, by the time he grabbed the food and fell back to lie on the ground, he had half of his bandages off. Bryan however, was too busy with his hunger and he neglected to see the signs that hinted of what the rest of the body had to say on the matter. Nor did he have time to mend the strips that had kept him from hurting. Instead, he quickly unwrapped the food without even reading the package, and devoured the whole thing in one bite. This did not satisfy his hunger however, nor end the exhaustion from moving so much, and so he ate until he was full.

One by one, he took the packages from the table and shoved them in his mouth. He did not even know what he was eating but whatever it was, it had never tasted as good as now.

When Bryan was back to his full senses, he could not move any more. His whole body was in a very fragile state, one which disguised itself and offered no pain but which started to hurt with even the slightest of motions. Even a small action like the blink of an eye hurt his whole body. He did not even know this was possible or even if his eyelids were in any way connected to his feet. But it did hurt, and so he had to reapply the strips by himself and also keep himself from any excess movement.

He tried closing his eyes but noticed that when he did, he fell asleep and the rest of his body would be wracked with pain if he moved while asleep. So, he opened his eyes and whenever his eyes started to tingle and hurt, he slowly blinked them making sure it wouldn't hurt.

The first hour or two was difficult but he at last got the hang of it. After he was content with his position on the floor next to the desk, he laid there with a smile on his face. Not because he was happy but because any other facial expression hurt the rest of his body.

Ever since he ate breakfast however, he could feel the sensation of having forgotten something that he could not pin point. He did not remember what he was forgetting nor if he was actually forgetting anything at all. His head was a blank, in fact, and he could not even remember what he did yesterday or when he fell asleep.

It was not unusual that he kept having a worry in the back of his head that he could not find a reason for. Most of Bryan's days had been such a repetition of events that it was not a big part of his thought process to recall what had happened the day before.

However, Bryan could sense that this time was different. It felt as though what he forgot must have been of great importance to him.

He lay there looking up, and through his peripheral vision he could see a smudge or something on the ceiling. Just then, he remembered the sign. He couldn't look at it at the moment but he remembered exactly what it said.

He was relieved for a moment thinking that he found what he forgot but he still had the mysterious worry that he just could not put a name to. He kept thinking and thinking until he heard an alarm. He looked over at the source and saw his clock ringing with a glowing red six and two zeroes on it. That was when he remembered everything.

'I have to get up and go to work.' Bryan thought.

Luckily, right before he went into the imbecilic series of actions of trying to get up, he was reminded by the sign on the ceiling. Still, even through his peripherals, it shined with its astonishing beauty and neatness. It stood there as if it was alive and looking at Bryan straight in the eyes. Almost as if it was telling

Bryan a message:

WILL BE BETTER IN A DAY OR TWO. DO NOT MOVE.

"Don't get up," he said.

'But it's been a day already. I should be able to get up. If I can't, I'm going to get fired. I don't want to get fired. No. I can't get fired. I don't have much money. If I do get fired, I only have enough money for a month's rent and for food, not even that.' Bryan was talking to the words as if they could actually understand him and respond.

After several moments of arguing with the inanimate series of curves and lines, he had to resolve himself to the inevitable truth. All he could do was lay there and do nothing. He knew he couldn't get up, not because the sign told him not to but because he really couldn't. He had used up all his energy while trying to retrieve his food. Not even the food that he had snacked upon would give him enough courage nor energy to get up.

Bryan turned his eyes toward his clock. The bright red light he wanted so much to comfort him was somehow gone. The clock was unplugged and the only thing that remained in its place was total darkness. Bryan sighed.

The sign had been right all along. He tried arguing with it but it always somehow won. Bryan knew deep down that it was no use. There was nothing that Bryan could do to make himself be able to move again at the moment. So, he would have to lose his job.

The worst part of it was that he did not even have a chance to explain to Mr. Johnson. He wished he had put the phone within hand's reach now that he could move his arms. Or at least, wished he had the overpowering desire like he had with the food, something capable of driving him to the phone. There was a slight chance that it would all still be okay if he called or not, but the main purpose of the call was for Bryan himself; Bryan thought maybe if he could explain the reasons, he would feel better about himself.

As for the moment, he felt useless. He felt that all he could do was blame all of this on himself. He knew that all this was his fault for he had made all the choices that had been made that day. However, he felt bad not for getting hurt, but for being saved by the woman. If he had died back then instead, it would have been painful but quick. Now, all he could do was wait until he got fired. Then he could wait until he ran out of money and starved. Then, he could wait until he died of starvation or until he got kicked out of his apartment and beaten again, possibly to death. All he was able to do now was to wait, wait and wait for his soon and coming death. This was worse than the pain he went through during his beating.

Just then, the phone rang. He turned his head over so quickly that with the sudden cracking of his neck bone latching back to position his neck started to hurt. This startled him because he was deep in thought. However, this pain was not of much significance right now for he had bigger issues. Unlike the day before, Bryan knew what was coming his way. It was about time. The slightly bright light coming from the window signaled that it must be around 11 o'clock already, the same time the first phone call happened before. He knew what and how much damage it was liable to cause. But most importantly, he was ready for it.

After a few long minutes of ringing, the phone switched to message and Bryan was able to make out a voice apart from a bit of buzzing. He heard his boss, angry out of his mind, screaming into the phone.

"Bryan, I am going to make this short so you can understand with your stupid human mind. Maybe this is shocking to you but, to be honest, I saw this coming. Even the first day you came to ask me for the job, I knew you would probably fail. But I felt sympathy for you. Ha! A San feeling sympathy for a human! Anyways, here it goes. YOU ARE FIRED," the message then ended with a loud beep. The beep rang in Bryan's head like a loud, high-pitched scream poking at his brain with the sole purpose of taunting him.

The last three words lingered in Bryan's mind. He

had gone through many emotions and thoughts in the past day or two and he thought in the end, he would be ready for the worst. He thought that he was willing to take whatever was coming his way because there was nothing he could actually do. But he was wrong. The last three words of that message repeated itself again and again inside of his head. It was like an eternal echo that was unstoppable inside the abyss of his mind. Like before, however, there was nothing he could do.

He was only human. Because he was human, he got into this trouble. Because he was human, there was only one-way for him to go, down. He couldn't get another job. There was no way for him to get money. The only thing he had now was the rest of the month in this apartment and a small amount of food which could not be replenished.

For the first time, Bryan actually felt nothing apart from his eyes tearing up at the sudden realization of how powerless he actually was. But he felt neither anger nor sadness. All he could feel was the pain from his wounds and his broken soul. At other times, he would usually feel anger toward himself or try to blame someone else, to make things better. But this was not like any other times. This time was actually a dead end. He did not have the time or the energy to spare to do those acts. He did not have the privilege of doing that, for all he had left was his life. If he had any money left to spare, he could move away like before. But for now, he was unemployed and could barely move. So, this time, there was no reason for him to feel anything.

There was no one to blame anymore, not even himself. There was no other way around it or any type of short cut to the solution of his so called problems. There was no way he could just make himself feel better by blaming it all on the fact that he was human. Yes, being human had its part in this but this was different.

He had always thought he was in trouble or that it was the end. He had not thought about what it would really feel like to actually be at a dead end, with nothing left to do with his life. It had never occurred to him that that there was an actual dead end, even worse than what he had imagined. He had not known that there could actually be such a place where he would have nothing left in his life but death. For example, he was ready to accept death a few days ago when he was beaten up. What he had not realized then was that he had had it good. He at least had had a job where he could get more money.

But now, he was running out of everything that was keeping him alive and he had no money. He was already living from paycheck to paycheck. Now he had nothing else in his life.

No matter what Bryan thought or said to himself, he could not get out of this nightmare. There was no sudden climax that would wake him up from this dream. His whole body was useless at the moment, and he himself had just turned useless as well. In fact, there was no use in feeling good about himself anymore. No matter what his emotions told him, he would still be on this down hill journey. For the first time in Bryan's life, he understood this.

Other times, the way he felt about himself was one of the most important things in his mind. Even if he felt that he was poor and ugly and useless, the process of it was still considered useful to him. Those self-evaluations were kind of like a clue to Bryan's competence. The very fact that he was able to think and see what was wrong with him was what pleased him, not when he felt that he was good at something.

No matter how unpleasant it was for Bryan, these things that used to be a big part of his life were not of any importance at all, and it was the truth. It was a stone cold truth. Life was simpler than Bryan had supposed. He was merely just another human in a San filled world, waiting for his death. Maybe, by chance, he would get lucky enough to survive for a few years but in the end, Bryan realized, he would end just the same as the man who'd thrown the egg.

There was nothing special after this realization.

The very next day, Bryan became better and could move again. He was first skeptical and pinched himself a couple times, figuring it was a dream, but he was soon to discover that he had gotten fired for something that would have been gone in just one more day. However, unlike what would have happened before, he did not get angry or sad at the knowledge, he just accepted it. He was going to die anyways.

He still felt a little awkward and his movement was a bit off, but as the days passed he was able to move freely again. He could kick his legs, run, jump and even skip but those abilities were no use to him now.

Every thing was pretty much back to normal. He woke up in the morning, ate breakfast, and did almost everything that he used to do. However, there was one major difference; he did not have to go to work.

This change in Bryan's life led to other major consequential events. For example, Bryan no longer woke up as early as he used to. He was also now able to eat three meals a day. Finally, he no longer left his house. He had no reason to.

He had no money to go out to buy food not did he need any more food. He was sooner or later going to get kicked out of the apartment for he only had the rest of the month left. Finally, there was no work place waiting for him in the day.

And so this new schedule was used for the rest of the month, until the landlord kicked him out.

Chapter 06

As Bryan left the building with his blanket and clock in hand, he could sense the dangerous path that now lay in front of him. He was now all alone, with no home and as always, no one to go to for help. Once again, he was hit with the dreadful thought that he could no longer be saved. There was no way a San would come and rescue him like before. That was just a one-time thing. It was all down hill from now on.

It was weird for him at first to see the outside world. It had been a bit less than a month since he had left his house. In fact, he hadn't left since the time he'd been beaten up. There was nowhere for him to go and everything he pretty much needed, or more like everything he could get, was already in his house. So he'd stayed in his house until he'd been evicted for not paying his rent.

Every thing else however, remained just the way it was. The sunlight was barely visible and above him the scarce sunlight was taken in by hundreds of Sans flying around and going about their business. If only Bryan had somewhere to go like all those people. But he didn't.

The bottom level of the entire city was still in bad shape and there was barely any room for him to walk even five steps to his side. There was trash everywhere and there were scraps and pieces of leftover food and wrappers that other humans and even Bryan himself had left.

Although all of this was so fascinating and it was good to be back outside, Bryan did not want much to do with any of it. He had just left his house for the first time in a month. It was great but it was not that significant considering the circumstances he was in. All Bryan wanted to do now was walk. In fact, all he could do right now was walk. He thought of all the possibilities of things that he'd thought he could do once kicked out of his home, but now he could not think of much. Walking was the most appropriate choice, it seemed. He thought by walking, he could take in the most of the place that he would be dying in, which for Bryan was a big deal. So, taking a deep breath he stepped off his doormat and turned right. He'd taken his first step.

Having no sense of where or how he was going to go anywhere, Bryan kept walking. He chose a direction and walked and walked until he reached a wall and then simply chose another point at which he did the same thing. The idea and desire to reflect back on his life and see as most of the city as he could were lost. There was no longer a purpose in this wandering. There was no destination waiting for him nor was there a reason in having all this exercise. This was just a way for Bryan to pass time until he hit the inevitable.

He did not look anywhere but straight in front of him. He did not stray off into his thoughts like he always did. He did not think back to his past. He thought of nothing and just kept walking. This was all he could do for now until he hit the inevitable wall that had been lined up for him ever since he was fired. That one event was the one thing that stayed in Bryan's mind. He was so engaged in this pointless walking that his mind went blank except for this one thing. However, it did not matter much.

This was because he knew it could not be changed and he was done denying it. He had known this fact the day he was fired. He was done with all the blaming and feeling bad for himself. He knew he would die, being outside with no home, either from starvation or from getting beaten up again. He knew this would happen so he felt that denying this would only make it worse.

'Maybe, I will die and be born again. Maybe in my next life, I will be San. Then I will have everything that I want in this life, in my next,' These were the thoughts that had haunted Bryan for almost every moment of the past few weeks.

Time passed, taking with it more and more buildings that Bryan had not even known were in the city until now. The buildings were not only becoming shorter, but had started to grow more apart, allowing more sunlight to filter down to the lower levels. If Bryan had known there was such a place as this before, he would not have decided to live in his crummy home with practically no sunlight. Still, the only thing in Bryan's mind now was the death he was expecting in the near future.

Paying no attention to where he was, Bryan kept a steady pace and kept walking. What Bryan did not realize was that the more he continued on with this steady walk, the better the condition of the streets became. More and more sunlight was let in as the buildings became more scattered, and there was practically no trash on the ground. It was obvious few other humans had been in this part of the city.

After about four hours of nonstop walking through the better part of the city, Bryan reached the end. He saw a small green sign with white letters saying:

YOU ARE NOW LEAVING SERVUSVILLE.

No matter how much it lured him and all the good possibilities that were no doubt possible there, Bryan felt no need to go outside the city unless it was the way to the human town. He had the same thoughts now that he'd had when leaving his last city and moving to this one. He felt like he could actually make a good life, and maybe be treated better than before. The only difference was the circumstances. The last time, he'd been in dire need of a move because the city was getting rid of its walking streets.

Only if he could actually reach a human town could he be saved maybe. But unfortunately, he was too far away from the human town, even being right on the border of the city. He would probably get beaten to death or die of starvation before he would reach the human town, being unable to fly.

So, he turned around and walked back. There was no regret, no wishing that if only he could fly or if only the human town were closer. He knew that there was no point.

Again, he was back to his pointless cycle of walking and turning and walking again. However, this time, he was less uptight and actually looked at things and thought on them. First he noticed how far he had gone from his house. Looking at his clock, he saw that he was three hours and forty-two minutes from his house. He has left his house at eleven and now it was two forty two. Secondly, he noticed that this part of the city was cleaner than the central parts. However, everything above him was the same.

There were still tall green tinted skyscrapers and many green skinned people flying high above. It was a miracle that he hadn't been attacked by a group of Sun Worshipers yet, for he had not cared to put on his green make that day. He thought either way he would end up the same and so had left his house, for the first time, leaving the unclothed parts of his body bare with no makeup whatsoever.

Although too caught up to notice before, Bryan was actually getting tired. Having nothing to fear and no place to go, Bryan decided to stop walking and sit down. He no longer had to run fast to stay away from any Sans. He didn't care.

He sat down in a relaxed position and leaned back onto a wall. He looked above him and watched the flying Sans in admiration.

"I'll be just like that in my next life," Bryan said to himself.

He noticed the amount of people above him were decreasing as time passed. Bryan looked at his clock. It was five thirty. It was about time the Sans would leave from work.

Bryan kept watching above him as less and less people were apparent and noticed that the sky was changing color as well. He knew right away that it would not be long until a few drunk Sun Worshipers would come along and see him. Then, he would be dead. Bryan had expected this to happen earlier, considering he was not wearing any make up. However, he knew that he could definitely count on the dark night to finish the deal.

Just then, a person wearing a Sun Worshiper head band landed not so far from Bryan. Bryan was caught off guard because he thought he would be safe until the sun was totally set. But he knew that it did not matter much any way and so just sat there waiting. He just sat there looking at the Sun Worshiper, expecting the worst.

However, nothing happened. This man just stood there fiddling with his keys to get into his house. It was unusual enough for a San to have a house on the first floor but a Sun Worshiper not attacking a human?

Bryan was not close enough to be seen in the dark, and so Bryan could not really see who this person was. Bryan was done waiting however, and decided to run and provoke the man himself. Maybe this person was too drunk to notice the nearby human.

Bryan ran over to the person. This worshiper seemed frustrated with his keys until he noticed Bryan standing next to him. He raised his head, observed Byran from head to toe, seemed to think to himself a little and smiled at Bryan. Bryan stood there petrified and feeling awkward as the San observed him.

Nothing seemed to fit anymore. This Worshiper was nothing like what he had expected. First of all, a Sun Worshiper was smiling at someone who was obviously human. What was even more confusing was that Bryan actually knew this person.

Bryan rubbed his eyes and looked at him again. He was right. This person was definitely the person he was thinking. He could never forget his face; what he had done had made such an impression on Bryan.

This Sun Worshiper was the very person who had thrown the egg at Mr. Servodeus. However, this time, his skin color was green, and he was flying rather than laying on the ground, half dead.

Bryan was confused. Was this Sun Worshiper truly the man who'd been human before? Or was he just a person that looked similar? He couldn't ask because if he was wrong, the Sun worshiper might kill him. Then again, that was his whole purpose for coming up to the person in the first place.

"Excuse me sir." said Bryan

"Yes? What do you want?" Asked the man. He

still had a wide smile on his face. The smile was pure and showed nothing but kindness. There was no condescension, nor any sense of humiliation attached to it. It was just pure, 'hello I am your friend' kind of smile.

"I know this might be weird but are you or are you not the person who threw the egg during the parade a month ago?" Bryan asked.

"As a matter of fact, yes I am."

"What? How? What happened?"

Bryan was confused. He was right about this man being the protester who'd thrown the egg but why was he not dead? This was all very unexpected. It did not matter much, but if the man was not dead because of the reason Bryan suspected, then Bryan's own problems could be solved.

"Come inside and I will tell you," answered the man.

The Sun Worshiper looked down at his keys and fiddled around. Bryan knew it would be hard for this man to see with almost no light. However, soon the door was opened and Bryan entered the house, led by the Sun Worshiper.

The Sun Worshiper turned on a light switch to his right as he entered the house. However, the light did not turn on right away but rather flickered on and off a few times before the lights were fully on.

Bryan, as he entered, looked around the room, expecting the best of the best because it was the house of a Sun Worshiper. However, even though it was better than his own, it was really not a good house at all. Even Bryan could tell.

The apartment was simply a big empty space with a bed, a desk and a clock and a few other frivolous objects. The walls were not in good shape and it was not clean at all. The only thing about it that was different from his own house was that it had a bed and more than one room.

The Sun Worshiper led Bryan to the desk and gave him a seat.

"So, first of all, what is your name?" asked the man.

"Oh, My name is Bryan." Bryan answered.

"No last name I suppose, being human and all. My name is Bob. I don't have a last name either because I was once human as well." He said.

"Okay, Bob, how did you become... like this?" Bryan straight to the point.

"They took me from the street to a camp and changed me. I am in fact collecting donations for the camp. Bryan the way, do you want to donate? It will of course be going to the camp" said the man as if this was obvious information.

"No. Sorry. But what is this camp you speak of?"

Bryan asked.

"Where have you been in the past month? This was all over the news. Haven't you heard of the camp Mr. Servodeus V has made to change humans into Sans? That's how I was changed." Answered the Sun Worshiper.

Bryan was shocked and all that was in his head was to get to the camp. Everything was aligned for him now. There would be no dying today. He would not die for at least a couple hundred years. He was saved.

"How do you get there?" Asked Bryan.

As soon as the man finished explaining the directions, Bryan got up and went straight for the door. However, the Sun Worshiper moved suddenly and stopped him in front of the door.

"Where are you going?" he asked.

"I have to go to this camp."

"If you go now you won't get there. There would probably be other Sun Worshipers out there that will probably kill you. Not all of the Sun Worshipers are as nice as me, you know. I'm just like this because I used to be a human. I know how you feel. You...uh..."

"Feel like there is nothing else to do in life but die?" Bryan finished the person's sentence for him.

"Yeah. That. But seriously, you should probably sleep here and go in the morning. I don't really care but if you want to, you're welcome."

"I guess you're right. If you let me I will sleep here and go in the morning."

"You can just sleep on the floor where ever you want." Bob said, moving over to the light switch and turning it off. The room got very dark and the only light that could be seen was a shimmering red glow from Bryan's clock.

Bryan set his blanket on a spot on the floor that was close to the door. Lying down, he folded half of the blankets over himself and closed his eyes. He waited and waited but nothing happened. He couldn't fall asleep.

Bryan twisted and turned until he found a comfortable position but still he couldn't fall asleep. He knew that if he wanted to sleep he had to stop thinking about tomorrow and what could happen.

But he couldn't. How could he? It would probably the most important thing that ever happened in his life. It would probably be the day he could at last turn into a San.

Bryan looked at his clock. He had set his alarm to five in the morning. He wanted to get to the camp as soon as the sun rose. The clock right now, however said 9:00. No wonder he couldn't fall asleep. It was way too early.

So, Bryan turned his body so that he was on his back and looking up at the ceiling. There was a dim red light that was shining on the ceiling so Bryan could actually see. This reminded him of the red writing that had been on his wall.

Bryan had neglected to erase the writing for he thought there was no use in erasing it. That writing probably saved Bryan's life but it had also lost Bryan's life. But now that Bryan thought back on this, if he hadn't been stopped in going to work that day, and had not lost his job, he might not have been able to meet Bob and learn about this camp.

So Bryan was thankful for the red writing and its writer, and for the first time in a long while, Bryan actually felt happy for his situation. Normally, the only time he was somewhat happy was when he was given a job to do by Mr. Johnson. Even that however, was nothing compared to Bryan's bliss now.

How could it be? He was going to achieve something he had wanted his whole life, to be a San. That was one little change that would change everything.

He would have a better life style. He would not die today. He would no longer have to be beaten up by the Sun Worshipers. Just thinking about these possibilities made Bryan happy because this time, it was actually possible.

Bryan looked over at his clock again. He wished time would go faster but it was still 9: 30. Bryan watched the clock as he longed for the minutes to change. He counted in his head sixty seconds but nothing would budge. Again and again he counted the seconds watching for any movement in the light. Still none.

'One two three...' Bryan thought, now for the fifth time.

The faster time goes, the faster he would be at the camp and then...

The mere thought of what would happen next gave him shivers and a grand smile across his face. The terror of getting fired just a few weeks ago was now so far away. His life was better than he thought.

With a content smile across his face and a good feeling to match it, he closed his eyes as he dozed off into sleep.

He dreamed the same dream in which he was a San. Except, this time, he was not chased by anyone nor did he fall into any abyss. It was a full and happy dream of being a San.

Chapter 07

The sound of the loud buzz as the clock signaled Bryan to wake up broke the silence that had existed for the last six hours. This did not startle Bryan much though, for Bryan had been awake for a long time. If it were any other day, Bryan would have swung his arms around trying to hit the off button of the clock, still half asleep and dreaming. However, today was different.

With only one swift motion, he quickly turned the alarm off and jumped to his feet. He made sure his landing did not make a loud noise as he hit the floor and peeked over to see if any of the noises had woken Bob up. It didn't. Bryan tiptoed around the room minding his business, still moving quietly and checking every once in a while to see if he had woken the other man up.

Bryan neatly folded his sheet into one square lump and put his clock right on top of it. After he made sure all his belongings were as neat as possible and would make the least amount of trouble for Bob, he headed for the door. One last time, he peeked to make sure Bob was not woken up as he grabbed the doorknob.

Bryan decided that if he were to become a San, he would no longer need those items, let alone need them in the camp. This would be his start to a new life. He felt a little bad that he couldn't leave a note of some sort of gratitude toward Bob but he thought that when he became a San, he could thank him then. And maybe, he would meet him at the camp. Besides, Bryan's handwriting was illegible.

As Bryan turned the knob and opened the door, a sudden rush of light came into the room. Luckily, his alarm had the right time in which the sun would rise. In this part of the city the sun was actually visible from the first floor. The street was bright and he could even see the sky, which was blue with almost no clouds.

Just outside the door, he looked back at his things one more time to check their neatness. He had made sure the sheet was folded and that the clock was set straight atop it. The red glow of the clock was still glimmering as Bryan closed the door.

'5: 36,' it said.

Bryan did not do any of his usual checks to see if a Sun Worshiper was near or bother with any of his other acts of cautiousness. He was going to be a San now and there would be no better time to act like one than now. He walked out the door proudly and went straight into a walk toward the camp. He didn't run or constantly look up to see if there was a Sun Worshiper above him, and most importantly, he was not even wearing his makeup.

The mere thought of becoming a San gave joy to him and overcame all his other weaknesses. His hunger from a full day's fasting was overshadowed and his fatigue from a full day's walk was not even felt. His mental state was better than ever and he was ready for whatever was on his way.

Unlike the day before, Bryan had a purpose in this walk. He was actually going somewhere. No matter how excited he was, he had to stop himself from running. This city was big and Bryan had only just gotten the directions yesterday from Bob. He could easily forget and if he got lost, his whole dream would be demolished. He would then probably be trampled by a group of Sun worshipers and possibly die.

Now that he actually had a chance to become a

San, all his memories of being human seemed so far away and he felt like he would miss it. His human circumstances had been with him since birth. That was almost twenty something years ago. During those years, Bryan had had many experiences. When he changed, he would be leaving all of it behind. It was not much but it was still what he'd spent his whole life with.

'I guess I'll miss this: the walking, the eating, the getting beat up, the getting fired, the getting beat up, wait. What am I thinking? No, I don't think I'll miss it at all.' Bryan said, quickly changing his mind. He smiled a little grin as he skipped along the walking space. There was nothing good in being human that he could miss. He had everything to gain but nothing to lose.

Bryan could not believe he had walked this far from his house. He hadn't noticed this yesterday but the walk seemed very long today. His excitement could only carry him for a short while, and after the first few skips and hops, Bryan went back to the walking that just never seemed to end.

It felt like he had been walking for hours but when he looked back on his path, he would be standing mere feet from where he'd been. Then he would jog in anguish but quickly get tired. This walk was just like the nightmare where he could not run away from the

Sun worshipers. But this time, he couldn't run away from his human state.

All of this was making him angrier, making him yearn more for his change. It was just all the more reason for him to quickly turn into a San and fly. Then, he could be where he wanted in less than five minutes, or not even that. Even if the destination was on the other side of the city. But thinking such things just made him even more frustrated with his circumstances in the here and now.

It was not even imaginable how much Bryan wanted to be a San. He had wanted to be a San, or at least not human, for almost all his life. He had even considered ending his life more than once in his brief stay in Servusville. He had considered it many times before as well, but never could get the necessary courage nor the will power to actually pull it off. The closest he had ever gotten to his death was when he had walked towards a group of drunk Sun Worshipers once before. But the worshipers were too intoxicated to notice and just flew away. After this, he had decided to stick with his life and took it as a punishment for a malicious past life.

Ever since Bryan could remember, he always believed his life to be only one of many lives that he could not remember. He always longed for a better life the next time, and regretted having such a horrid life in his past to have caused him to have such a terrible one in the present.

But, Bryan could not stop himself from still longing for a better path in his current life. Every night, he dreamed about this chance and vowed to give anything to catch it if it was given to him. If offered, he would take his chance even if it meant he would die soon. It was that important to him. And this time, it was right in front of his face, and unlike his dreams, he had nothing to lose, just like one other time he could recall being so close.

In fact, the situation Bryan was in right now was just like the one when he was thirteen. He had been taken into the orphanage house and was able to wait there until he could take the new injection. Although he could still proudly say that the time he had then was the most comfortable experience he had ever had in his life, it had still failed. And because of this, Bryan still had a sense of worry in the back of his mind.

But he kept telling himself, "This time, it's different. There is proof. Bob was turned into a San."

And yes, there was no doubt about that. Bryan had even slept in the house of a person who had actually gone through the procedures he was looking for. There was no other reasonable explanation. If Bob were not a participant of the new vaccine, why would a Sun Worshiper let a human sleep in his house and tell him directions to a Sun Worshiper base camp? And, why would a San throw an egg at Servodeus, the king of all the Sans?

"Bob had said that as long as one goes into the camp and waits for his turn, there is a hundred percent chance of him becoming a San." Bryan said to himself.

"And this came from a person who was actually a part of it, so it must be true."

'He said that they made a new vaccine. Instead of the N1E2, they changed the composition or something. He said that they found the problem. He said...they made a (think of new name)' Bryan thought to himself as he pushed on towards the camp.

Bryan's dream, ever since he found out about the two classifications of people, was about to come true. With just a little time, for the first time in his life, he would be treated like an actual thinking being, not a poop head or a crap monkey or a human, but an actual San. A normal San of the San world. He would not have to be the "special" thing people looked down upon any longer.

And this was staring at him in his face. All he had to do was walk over to the camp and wait his turn. Bryan was already set upon the first step.

The only thing that Bryan could ask more of this beautiful perfect day was for this walk to be shorter. But Bryan knew he couldn't fix that. He didn't have the power, not yet, at least.

It didn't even matter. It all ends up the same and the only endings are the best ones Bryan could ask for.

After almost an hour of walking Bryan was beginning to get tired. There was a lot on Bryan's mind and it was hard for him to walk like yesterday when his mind had been adrift. He was full of excitement and anticipation now, and the more he wanted to get to the camp, the longer the walk seemed.

At last, Bryan had to stop to catch his breath. He picked the cleanest spot on the polluted streets and walked over to it. He could barely breathe right now from the constant rotation of walk, jog, run, skip and then walking again. He supported his upper body with his arms against his knee as he bent over to sit on the curve. But just as he was about to sit down on the curb before a random house, he noted that a large metal structure was visible, only about three hundred yards away. It was a metal door, shining with heavenly glimmer as it reflected all of the light that could be caught upon the first level.

As soon as Bryan saw this he instinctively got up and started running. He could feel how tired he was inside but no matter how much he tried to tell his body to stop running, his body kept moving, running on by itself. His subconscious self had told his body to run and Bryan could not do anything about it.

There was so much energy churned up inside him that he could no longer be contained or forced to walk. But as Bryan got closer to the structure, a thing still glimmering with a ominous shine, he could see he did not have to walk anymore. He could not get lost when he was that close.

Just in front of the door, he stopped and fell down on the ground. With the last bit of energy he had left, he lifted his arm up in the air as he screamed in relief. He was there.

There was a large metal door with a large Sun worshiper symbol on it, a green sun. The door was completely made of metal and was shining steel-grey all over except for the sun. The Sun was drawn in rubber-based paint and gave off no luster even though the wall was so shiny. The door was so big. It was at least two stories high and one building width of length. Along the whole top of the door and walls that were next to the gate hung barb wire twirling like vines with spikes and a red margined white sign separated by five feet of wire that said:

WARNING: ELECTRICITY

Bryan only rested for a few seconds to admire the door and then got up to press a doorbell. He could feel his legs twitch in exhaustion but he kept himself up and looked for a button.

He found and rung the doorbell located in the

middle of the large sun. He had to stand on his toes and reach his hand high to press it. Obviously, this door was built for Sans who could simply fly up to the door bell.

There was a long buzz following the press, like a phone ringing. Then there was a voice. It was not visible where the voice or the buzz was coming from but it seemed to come from almost all directions.

"Name please," Asked the voice.

"I am Bryan. I am a human and I am here because a frie....I mean someone told me that I could get the new vaccine here to turn into a San." Answered Bryan as he panted between every word. Bryan was so busy catching his breath that he almost said that Bob was his friend. But luckily, he stopped himself. He couldn't say that Bob was his friend because he had just met him. Also, he was a San.

"Come in" the voice said. Then, there was large slamming noise as if the person on the other side of the phone threw the phone down while hanging up.

Right as the voice ended, the gate started to open. The door split in two parts right along the middle of the sun and the doorbell in the middle was taken along with the left door with a round bump. The two wall-like gates slid into the surrounding buildings on each side and Bryan could feel the ground shake as the two great walls scraped against each other. The massive things slid across the ground as if by magic.

The door itself was a spectacle but what was behind it was even more amazing. Inside was the largest open area Bryan had ever seen in his life.

Bryan counted a line of 25 cabin-like houses on each side and stretching for as far as Bryan could see. All these houses had a similar door to the main gate, each with a green sun on it. In the large open area between the two lines of cabins were Sun Worshipers marching in a group like an army and training as if there was going to be war. All of these worshipers were armed with a rifle and were wearing green camouflage suits from head to toe except for the white part of the headband. Even their boots were green leather.

On the far end of the open area was a large castle-like building painted all in green with a fancy gate and structure much like the president's house that Bryan had once seen a picture of in the orphanage. Bryan could not believe that he did not notice this place being built. This was not only close to his house but it had obviously started long before he'd been stuck in his home.

'So this was the thing Servodeus was talking about on the interview,' he thought.

As Bryan gazed in awe at the Sun Worshiper base camp-slash-human change camp, a Sun Worshiper came out of a small container box type object right next to the door and came up to Bryan. The small container box had windows on each side and inside were a bunch of electric things, which seemed difficult to handle to Bryan.

"Hey." Said the person. He was visibly irritated and obviously did not want to be there.

Bryan could immediately tell that this person was the voice which Bryan heard from the bell.

"Yes?" he said.

"Yeah. Lets go. You're human right? Come on. Let's go. Hurry up," said the worshiper.

Without a word, Bryan followed him as he led him to one of the houses. He was led to the second house on the right side. On the house door, there was the same exact symbol as on the others, except instead of a bell; there were large letters written on it. Bryan made out the letters and numbers on the door to be;

M24

"Okay here is your house. Get in." Said the man as he quickly flew back over to the container box.

The door was automatic and as Bryan stepped closer the door swung open almost hitting Bryan, who'd been expecting the door to be like the main gate, which slid. He walked into the room not expecting anything special but he was struck by something even less.

Inside the cabin were two lines of bunk beds, one

on each side with people lying on it. Nobody was speaking to anyone else, let alone trying to speak with the new person. Everyone was reading a different book and once in a while, Bryan could see a person peeking up to look at Bryan. But as each made awkward eye contact, they would quickly turn back to their book and turn in the other direction.

The room was quiet and the only sound that was barely heard was the sound of turning pages and people breathing. The room did not seem like the happy place Bryan had expected from people who would soon be changing into better, stronger beings.

Nobody was at all excited like Bryan was to be sleeping in a bed, nor did they seem excited to be turning into a San. Bryan did not want to look weird so he had to keep a straight face in turn. It was hard though because he was ecstatic in expectation of his new life. He would even be happy if he was kept here forever and not turned into a San. This was the good life. He even had a bed.

On the far side of the cabin was a bookshelf that covered he whole back wall of the cabin, every inch of it filled with books. Each and every person there was holding a book and were either sleeping or reading.

Close by, next to the door in the left corner, there was a bucket and a roll of paper.

Bryan picked an empty bunk, the furthest he could

find from the waste area, and went over to the bookshelf to pick out a book. He did not like reading nor did he normally ,try reading books but because of the peer pressure from his cabin mates, he felt he had to. It was not the first thing on his mind but he did not have anything else to do.

He brought the book over to his new bed and lied down. He put his head against the soft pillow and flipped to the first page.

He hadn't read many books in his life and so he did not know how to pick a fun book. He had just picked the first in sight.

"Adventures of Bob," it said on the cover.

Bryan could barely understand the first few sentences on the first page. It was not that the words were too hard, but he couldn't read it.

"Bob was walking down the street. He was the only one walking..." The first two lines read.

It was hard for Bryan to read because until today, he had never read more than three sentences at once. However, because he knew when he became a San, he would need to be able to read well, he persisted.

The more he read, the better he got. After couple hours of reading, he was finally on the thirtieth page and he actually understood what was happening in the story.

Suddenly, a large buzzing noise alarmed him and

he quickly threw his book on his bed. He regretted this because it would be hard for him to find his page again.

He looked around in puzzlement as one by one, the others in the cabin marked their place in their book and got up. They all got in a neat line like a bunch of zombies in front of the door.

Without knowing where this was leading, he got in the back of the line and followed the rest of the people out and into the large fancy castle-like house at the end of the field. He thought this would be the time they would all get the new vaccination.

As the group passed the other cabins, one by one, other groups started to come out of each cabin door and started to add on to the already large group. Every one of them stood in a neat line and every one of them was human. But still, nobody talked to anyone else. Not even with the person in front of them. There were no whispers nor were there any salutes to any of their friends.

Bryan had never seen so many humans in one spot before. The most he'd ever seen previously was three, but that was in a human specialty store. Nobody spoke as they approached the large building and entered through the door.

The inside of the castle was even more amazing then the outside. The floor was covered with granite and on the walls were pictures of people and scenery. In every corner where a wall met another, there was an antique object, some of which Bryan could have sworn were sold from the shop he worked at. For example, the red automobile was there. There were three hallways leading from the door and front room. There was the grand hall way straight ahead with just as many decorations as the front room, and a hallway that led left which was not so beautiful as the others but rather empty, its walls, floor and even the ceiling all painted white. Then, there was the right hallway. This hall was barely even cleaned and Bryan could even see large amounts of mold in the corners where the walls met the floor.

Unfortunately, where Bryan was going was to the right. As soon as they entered the door, they turned right and into the long hallway that awaited them. There were many doors on each side of this hall way but they were all passed one by one until at last the throng entered the door on the very far end.

On the other side of the door was a large enclosed area with many tables. On the right side of the room was a long table with all sorts of wrapped food, looking much like what was found in the specialty store, and on the left side were many tables and seats so anyone could choose to sit anywhere.

Everyone got into two lines, with one line for each

side of the food table. Bryan was in the middle of his line and was probably going to get the worst of the foods offered. He was worried all the good food would be taken by the time he got to the table. However, this did not matter much to Bryan because he was still happy just from the fact that he would be a San in a short while.

It did not take as long as Bryan had expected to get his food. He picked out the ones that he had tried before and knew to be good, and then headed towards the other tables.

He looked around considering where to sit but just then, he heard someone whisper his name. Everyone who had taken a seat was already seated quietly, but there was a large blowing noise from above the door due to the air conditioning. Bryan decided that he had just been hearing things then, and so kept looking around for someone he may at least have seen before to sit with, but he couldn't find anyone.

So, having no other choice, he went straight to the closest available seat.

"Bryan," he heard again, this time a bit clearer.

Bryan looked up toward the call but still did not see any familiar faces. He then sat down and just as he was about to open his first package of food, he felt a tap on his shoulder. He looked up and saw that the person tapping on his shoulder was none other than the girl he had met at the parade. The only human friend he knew in the whole city.

"I've been calling you. Bryan, right?" said the girl.

"Yes. Uh...what are you doing here?" asked Bryan.

"Come. Follow me. You must be new here right?" she said.

"Yeah. I just came here this morning."

Bryan followed the girl and sat across the table from her.

"So. I'm just glad there is someone I know here now. I just got here like a week ago. It's so boring here. What are you doing here?" the girl asked. She was obviously excited to find a friend.

"What? When are we getting the new injections? This is the place right?" Asked Bryan. Bryan was too concerned with the whole injection process to hear anything else from her.

"Okay." A little irritated from Bryan's cluelessness, she began again. This time a little slower with a deliberate pause between every word. "I got here about a week ago. Yes I wanted to be a San. And you want to know when you become a San? That all depends on what cabin you are in. I, for example, am in cabin F 25. It's probably going to be a while until I become a San. The injections are given based on what cabin you are in. It starts in M1 then F1 then M2 and so on. What cabin are you in?"

"Me? I'm in M24. So I will probably be before you and it will be a while until it's my turn. I guess."

"And there is breakfast, lunch and dinner here and there's...."

Another buzz interrupted their conversation. Then, like in the cabin, everyone got up and headed for the door.

"You get the picture. I have to go, so I'll probably see you later. It's good to have someone you know here. I've been all alone for the past week. Okay bye. I'm Jennifer by the way," She quickly said as she got up and headed for the door.

Bryan had been so busy listening to Jennifer that he had forgotten to eat. He quickly opened the two wrappers and shoved them in his mouth. He got up and ran for the door hoping to meet Jennifer again but she was gone.

Bryan followed the crowd back to his cabin and returned to his book. In his book, Bob was being beaten up by a bunch of his friends.

After another three hours of reading, the now familiar buzzing noise announced that it was time for lunch. Bryan folded the bottom of the page he was on and headed out the door. This time, he knew that the later he went to the dining hall, the less food and time for him to eat, so he went through the crowd quickly and cut toward the front.

Once again, he got his food and went for a table. But just as he was about to sit down, he stopped himself and looked over at the line to look for Jennifer. There she was waving at him. She ran over to Bryan without even getting her food, and brought him over to the same table they'd sat at before and sat him down.

"Wait here," she said.

Then she went back to the end of the line. Bryan, remembering how he'd barely finished his food the last time, took the chance while Jennifer was waiting in line and ate all of his food. That way he could have a full stomach and be able to talk to someone he knew, He was lucky really, most of people in this camp didn't seem to know anybody. They weren't even willing to get to know anybody, it seemed. But now that Bryan actually knew someone, he felt it would be much better while waiting his turn for the vaccine.

Soon, Jennifer came back holding two packages of food and took a seat sat across the table from Bryan. Unlike the conversation after the parade, this time, it did not end after just a few words.

Chapter 08

Three days passed and Bryan waited his turn for the injection. Just like his old life, everyday was the same. Without even being told so by his no longer available alarm clock, Bryan got accustomed to waking up at seven thirty. He would read his book for about an hour or so and then he would go and eat breakfast. Breakfast, lunch and dinner were all located in the dining room and always consisted of the same instant hot dogs and other products.

At breakfast, he always sat with Jennifer. Even after three days, Bryan could not find anyone else to socialize with and so he stuck with her. After the first day or so, they actually used up every subject they could talk about. For example, Bryan was done asking her questions about the camp after the first two meals. But still, having an acquaintance to accompany him was good.

The time after breakfast was pretty much designated for his reading. Bryan had just finished "Adventures of Bob" and now he was going for a second book.

He enjoyed the book, although he wasn't able to understand much of it due to his poor comprehensive skills. From what he could make out though, he found that the story was much like his life here, and he learned from Bob's mistakes. He learned never to take chances like Bob did when he walked on the weak rope bridge, a choice which led to his death.

But by the time he finished his first book, he was more fluent and was able to read at least a page in a minute, although he still wasn't able to understand most of it. He sometimes had to return to an already read page and read it again and again until he could barely understand the plot line and simply had to go on with the next page.

After the reading, he would eat lunch with Jennifer and do some more reading. Then, at about three o clock, the people would be allowed to go outside for about thirty minutes. Surprisingly, everyone, including Bryan, would stay inside instead. He had thought about leaving every day since he had entered the cabin, but he could not bring up the courage to act alone in front of all these people. Most likely because he did not know them.

Everyone else seemed to be afraid of the Sans marching outside, as was Bryan himself But Bryan knew, or at least he thought he knew, that the Sun Worshipers were nicer now than they used to be. Bob was like that, so Bryan figured, the Sun Worshipers must be changing.

After this "outside" period, Bryan read again. With all the reading he was doing, Bryan was now able to finish the thousand page books even faster than he had finished the thin book he had started with.

Then, he would go to dinner. Usually, by dinnertime, Jennifer and Bryan would both be pretty tired and would stay quiet. They would both stare down at their food fiddling around with it. They never before had had three meals a day and were not hungry by the time the third meal arrived. Directly after, Bryan went to sleep. The days were so monotonous that he was having more fun either reading or sleeping than anything else.

All the while, each day, he heard that ten people from the first few cabins would be taken. Ten were taken from each male and female side of the camp. In the mornings, all these people, as when they went to the meals, would go in a line into the main building. Instead of turning right however, they would turn left and enter the first door on their right. In there, no one knew what happened. But Bryan would always imagine and even dream about what was taking place in that room.

He knew that people went into that room because he saw them go in when he left for breakfast. Whenever the door was opened though, all Bryan saw was a brief glimpse of bright light coming from it.

There was a rumor though, that when they entered through that door, that there was a whole other room filled with delicious food that no human would ever see until it was their turn. It was the type of food that only Servodeus and his followers would be privileged enough to eat. On the table would be things that Bryan could not even begin to imagine. Things that, maybe, were never even wrapped in the instant plastic bags that food always came in.

It was said that that the meal was supposed to be their last meal as humans, and therefore the Sans were generous enough to give them a meal that they could remember. Although this was not what Bryan thought a San would do, he was reminded of Bob and how nice he was to him, and therefore considered it a possibility.

Even though the life was monotonous, everything

in the camp was new to Bryan and he did not mind it overmuch. The beds, the free food, and even being around so many people in the same situation he was, was all new to him and distracted him from any boredom. Especially, this was far better than the few privileged days he had spent in the orphanage when he was thirteen. The mere fact that there was a guarantee for him to become a San drove him through those boring days with hardly a care on his mind.

All the while, everyday, Bryan searched for Bob. Bob had been very hospitable to him and he wanted to thank him. He knew that Bob must come to this camp once in a while. After all, he was a Sun Worshiper. So on the fourth day, Bryan decided to try going outside during the outdoor period. He thought that maybe the reason he couldn't find Bob was because he didn't try looking there.

After a couple hours of reading, Bryan looked up as he always did to rest his eyes. He looked around the room with a cautious glance just waiting for someone to stand up before him and go outside. No one did. Instead, he made awkward eye contact with someone across the room from him. Both of them quickly set their eyes back to their books.

Five minutes passed and no one left. Ten minutes. Fifteen. Still nobody.

Right when Bryan saw the clock hanging above

the door turn to three twenty, he got up. He had been waiting this long for someone to go out, and so decided that he had to be the first person everyone was probably waiting for. Bryan got up and headed straight for the door. He could feel the admiring eyes behind him as he left the room.

He didn't look back and he just walked straight to the field. Actually, it wasn't even a field. The ground was all covered in asphalt and in the middle of the empty area, there was a huge green sun painted. It was much like the giant gate Bryan had seen days earlier.

He walked around a little bit, tracing the giant circle of the sun and enjoying the sunlight as he looked for the line of soldiers he always noticed. One by one, behind him, he could see people from his cabin come out. First peeking their heads out and then their bodies. Bryan felt the satisfaction grow inside of him, for he had just led a group to follow him. He didn't have time to pay much attention to them though, as he only had ten minutes now to find Bob. Then again, the field was very open and hopefully, it would be relatively easy.

Bryan couldn't believe that it was only four days since he'd come here. It seemed much longer since he'd arrived. All the while though, he was waiting for the line with Bob in it.

Just then, Bryan heard the marching of at least a few dozen-soldier boots clanking against the asphalt ground. Bryan turned around and brought his hand over his eyes to block the sunlight and there, Bryan could barely see as he squinted, there was Bob, standing in the first row first column with the serious, no-nonsense look of a soldier. Bryan wasn't sure at first because of all the sunlight, not being very accustomed to it as he'd only lived in the shadowy part of town for the last year or so, but Bryan was so excited to see Bob; he didn't care if it wasn't him.

Being a newcomer and all, Bryan did not know any rules regarding how to act near the Sun Worshiper soldiers. He no longer believed in the rules he'd followed in the outside world, for his ideology had crashed when he'd met Bob a few nights ago. He now believed since he was soon to become a San, that he was equal to the Sun Worshipers.

He didn't even bother to ask Jennifer for any of the rules. He simply thought it was okay to just run over there, and thus Bryan did so in great excitement.

However, none of his excitement paid off. It was not that anyone stopped Bryan and sent him off to his cabin, and nor was it that Bryan had mistaken another person with all the sunlight. But what startled him was that no one welcomed him either. Bryan stumbled to a confused stop as he almost collided with the marching soldiers. Without even noticing him, they kept marching; they did not even flinch at a human coming at them full speed.

Bryan waved his hands in front of Bob and called his name multiple times in frustration. But still, the man did not answer. Bob kept marching in the weird steps of a Sun worshiper. Bob was marching and brought his leg straight up in a ninety-degree angle at every step, never bending it. It seemed silly to Bryan but who was he to judge them?

Bryan jumped around yelling Bob's name as he struggled to keep up with the crew. His former, cautious self was gone and his frustration at his "friend" not recognizing him kicked in.

At last, out of exasperation and exhaustion, Bryan stopped his chasing and decided to head back to his bunk. Bryan tapped Bob in the arm as he said good bye and turned to go back to his cabin. Bryan did this gesture friendly enough, yet perhaps less cautious or aware of the fact that he was still human and Bob was a Sun Worshiper.

He did not expect anything to happen when he tapped Bob lightly with the palm of his hand, already seeing that Bob did not respond to any other attempts at communication.

But at the exact moment Bryan touched him, Bob turned his head and stared at Bryan in a condescendingly angry look that even showed signs of violence. He even stopped, and behind him, a line of twenty or so soldiers all halted in a military stance, with one un-coordinated stomp on the ground, each of them still looking up at a forty five degree angle into empty space.

"Get away from me, you crap head," Bob said with sincerity.

And with one swift motion, Bob shoved Bryan back into the empty air and started marching again. Bob acted as if nothing happened and now was again marching with the empty face of a soldier as he moved on with the rest of the worshipers.

On the ground ten feet from where he'd been standing, bruised and scraped up from the push, Bryan got to his feet and moved back to his cabin as quickly as he could. This would be the last time he would have anything to do with Bob.

Bryan did not tell anyone about this incident, not even Jennifer. He had talked to her about Bob and how he was like a friend to him, but it was good now that he had not told her that he was going to find him that day because then he would have to tell her what happened. He did not understand this event enough to tell anyone yet. Maybe, when he was ready, he would.

Chapter 09

Without the incident even being mentioned, days passed. Gradually, the memory of it was beginning to fade from his mind as days, weeks and then even months passed by like the hands on a clock. Bryan could sense his own turn coming up soon. Every day passed by insignificantly but at the same time, he was that much closer to becoming a San. After all, that was the sole reason he lived.

Even now the routine of ten people from each gender line being taken continued, with the sequence currently stuck in the tenth cabin or so. It was about half way to the point where Bryan would get his injection.

The days were monotonous and Bryan could barely even tell which day of the week it was at this point, let alone the actual date. He was now on his fourth book, being at the point where he could read a book in less than a week with all the time he had. He was able to understand the material more completely and could make out the symbolism and deeper meanings to the text as well as the story itself.

Apart from the fact that he could read better, everything else about life in the San camp remained the same. He would wake up, eat, read, eat, read, eat, and then he would go to sleep. All through the meals and now sometimes during the times outside, he would be with Jennifer, hanging out just for the sake of having a friend. Other than such kindness, he was driven only by the thought of becoming a San. Without this guarantee, Bryan would probably not have been able to withstand all the boredom and fruitless cycle of life in the camp.

However, one thing was definitely different with Bryan. He was now closer to Jennifer in a way than he'd ever felt before. She was the only actual friend he had. Bryan used to think that Bob had been his friend, but had been proven disastrously wrong on that score months ago. But this time, it felt different. It was not the same feeling he had when he'd thought he was friends with Bob. He didn't know exactly what was different but he knew something was. Bryan just didn't know what.

It was unclear to Bryan until the point where it was only two cabins away from being his turn.

That day, just like always, Bryan went down to the breakfast area expecting Jennifer's always flamboyant greeting. Jennifer was now a big part of Bryan's life. She was his only friend and she made his life much easier in the camp. She was like a partner heading for the same goal. Bryan was relieved by her presence everyday upon this journey. With her, he never felt like he was the only person who had to walk this road. He became less afraid about the injection.

With her always-smiling face and cheerful attitude, she usually took up most of Bryan's day. But on that particular day, she looked very serious and seemed as though she had something on her mind.

Bryan greeted her with a normal, everyday hello, expecting a more boisterous reply. She didn't answer. Bryan then brought his food and sat down next to her. Still, there was no reply.

Bryan was used to receiving the silent treatment from other Sans so he stopped trying and ate his food. But suddenly, out of nowhere, Jennifer started talking.

"Bryan, you know we are really good friends right?"

"Yeah" Bryan replied, a little confused.

"Well, I've been thinking. How much are you willing to give up for this relationship? I mean, what's the limit?"

"..." Bryan couldn't reply. He just didn't understand what she was talking about.

"Alright, don't answer. Just listen. You see, I've been thinking and I thought up a crazy idea that you and I might not be just friends. I don't know. I've never really felt like this. But anyways, I know we're friends and everybody knows that once you become a San, you lose emotions and...."

Bryan now caught on with what she was saying. But what was she talking about with the less emotions thing? Everything started to kind of make sense.

"That's why Bob was like that to me!" Bryan shouted.

Jennifer was surprised by this out of the blue comment but she just kept going with what she had in mind.

"Okay... Well anyways, I don't really think we should go through the whole process of becoming a San anymore. I don't know."

Now, Bryan was puzzled.

'What is she talking about? What? Not change? I don't get it....'

"Well breakfast is over, so I guess I'll see you

during lunch. Think about it will you?" Jennifer said as she left the room.

Bryan stayed there, still petrified at just the mere thought of doing what Jennifer had suggested. Soon, one of the Sun Worshipers had to tell him to leave, and the Sans were not happy. They seemed ready to use violence when Bryan suddenly obeyed them and quickly ran back to his bunk. There, rather than reading like he used to, he just sat and stared into the open space between him and the ceiling. Blank. He had nothing on his mind. He didn't want to think about it. He didn't want it to be true at all.

Chapter 10

Days passed and Jennifer and Bryan did not meet together for meals any longer. Bryan still needed time to think it all over and the decision was just too hard for him to make.

Some days, he would accidentally run into her but Jennifer was every time kind enough to sit somewhere else to give him some space. She wanted an answer but she did not want him rushed. She knew as well as Bryan that it was a difficult decision to make. She knew because she had had to make the same decision before she could ask Bryan. Except, she knew she was not as enthusiastic for the injection as Bryan was. For

Bryan, the injection was his life's goal. If he hadn't found out about it three months previous, he would have killed himself. The promise of the injection was what had stopped him. The moment Bob told him of the camp, he'd made his choice.

But now, Bryan knew one more thing had become a huge part of his life. The two things he had to choose between were probably the most important facets of his life. He needed both. Jennifer was his only friend now that Bob was gone, and he liked her more than he liked anything else. It was a different feeling than just the friendship he'd felt with his mates in the orphanage long ago. It felt like nothing he'd encountered before.

Days became weeks and weeks turned into the passing of a whole month. The decision had to be made soon because his turn was approaching. Bryan no longer lay in his bunk reading books but instead just sat there staring out into open space trying to think of a solution to his problem. He stayed up late into the night staring at the ceiling. Bryan skipped most meals now, preferring to stay in bed. When he did eat, he ate very little. He was just too engulfed by the thoughts that would change his entire life.

One choice would take him in one direction, while the other would take him in another. Still, he had not talked to Jennifer about any of this. For now it was just a cycle of thoughts in his head, each fighting for dominance. One would defend Jennifer while one would defend Bryan's childhood and life long dreams.

Bryan had grown up not knowing anything of Jennifer and he would not have cared at all for her if it weren't for him being here. But he had grown up with the knowledge of the classifications of the world, and ever since he could remember he'd longed for the higher position in the hierarchy that the Sans were privileged enough to have. How were those people any better that Bryan? Why did they deserve the better life while Bryan does not?

'Is it because they have better genes?' Bryan thought.

'No, there are human children born from Sans parents.'

'Is it because the Sans are more amiable or even generous and deserve it morally?'

'No. Those same San parents mercilessly throw away their children and feel neither grief nor remorse. There is no sympathy towards the "monkeys" and even if there were any, there are none who are courageous enough or feel sympathy powerfully enough to act upon it.'

No, there was no reason for Bryan to give up on the dreams he'd long held. He had just as much right as Bob or even Servodeus to get the powers and privileges of life he desired.

Just when Bryan would finish thinking up this elaborate description as to why he should get the injection, he would remember something Jennifer had said, or merely think of her in general, and in doing so he would forget it all.

Was it not Jennifer who made his wait in this camp bearable? She was his only friend and Bryan would do almost anything for her. But now he had to choose if he really could do anything for her, even if it included giving up his life-long dream.

It was just too hard to choose. It was true that the Sans did not treat him well when he was a human, and Bryan knew he should feel mad at the Sans. He should feel angry at them and maybe even feel that the Sans were dirty or impure and that he himself should not want to become one of them.

But the thought of a better, longer, and stronger life was not that simple to give up. So what if the Sun Worshipers beat Bryan close to death multiple times? So what if because of the Sans, Bryan had had to live a life of shame and always had to feel as though he were a failure? He had to think about it from the other perspective.

It was true, the Sans were better than Bryan. This did not mean that they were better than him since birth, but what they lived with thereafter; yes, they were stronger, and economically more powerful than Bryan.

They could live longer and do more things than Bryan could dream of. This was all true.

Also, was it not true that Bryan would have done the same if he had been in their situation? He could say no right now, and state that he would be nice to all people "lower" than him, treating them as equals. He could say this to try to seem nice to himself and better than the other Sans. But he would be lying if he said it.

It was obvious that he would be mean and condescending towards humans if he were a San. That was one of the things Bryan was looking forward to. Having a complex enough brain to understand completely who one is compared to the rest of the world is something only humans and Sans had developed. No other animals or living creatures had developed this talent, skill or curse. Because of this, humans wanted more and more, always seeking higher positions in this world of hierarchies. Because Bryan was human, he was not perfect and so wanted to prove his high level in society by comparing himself to ones he knew to be lower than him. Consequently he knew he would treat other humans in just the same way other Sans had treated him.

So, Bryan couldn't blame the Sans and Sun Worshipers for the malicious acts they had committed. He knew he would do the same if he were in their position.

But why did it matter? Even if Bryan would have done the same, was it not still wrong and shouldn't Bryan still be mad at them?

If Bryan could simply just sustain his anger towards the Sans until deciding to not take the injection, everything would be over. He could keep his friend and he could be happy.

But sooner or later, Bryan knew that he would regret it, and would begin to think "what if?". That was just the way it was.

He started to hate Jennifer. Why did she have to be here in the camp with him?If only she weren't tere, he would just get the injection and leave. Why did she have to be in the camp at the same time he was? They could have met later on after they had became Sans. It would not be the same then as it was now though. Bryan now knew that Sans lost the ability to love someone or care for anyone but themselves. He had learned that the hard way through Bob.

But maybe it could be different for he and Jennifer.

The whole injection and becoming a San was all Bryan had lived for everyday of his life. Before he even knew about the camp, he had dreamt of opportunities just like this and even of the future after the injection where he was able to fly and live in an actual house.

This was all he had dreamed of ever since he could remember. There were many different versions of the dream, where some became nightmares and some became happy ones but all the same, they all started with him being a god.

To Bryan's eyes, Sans were gods. No matter how much they tormented him or beat him up, or perhaps because of that, they had always been that way to him. They were able to do anything: things that Bryan could barely even think of, Things that Bryan would never be able to do if he chose wrong and things Bryan had looked up to all his life. Incredible things that had birthed Bryan's interest in Sans. And all Sans in the world, without exception, were capable of doing those things.

It was not that Bryan wanted to be above every one in the world and show off to crowds of non-existant friends. No, he just wanted to do what everyone else was able to do before Bryan could even walk.

He wanted to jump off buildings and not get hurt. He wanted to go for days without any food. He wanted to live in his own house with a bed or even be able to reach one of the top stories of a house with his own strength. Bryan wanted to fly around the whole city, seeing everything in only one day. Most importantly, he wanted to walk a street without the fear of getting attacked by a gang of Sun Worshipers.

Bryan was sick and tired of simply regretting his misfortunes. He was sick of calling Servodeus bad names in his mind and he was tired of not being able to do what he wanted just because he was human. And now, there was a chance right in front of him, with not even a week away before his turn, a chance for him to turn his whole life around. He would be able to do everything he ever wanted then. But now someone, a person he hasn't even known for half a year yet, was telling him to give this all away? It had to be very easy to choose. It should have been easy to choose the injection. But why wasn't it?

'Why can't I just choose what I wanted for my life? This is what I wanted. I haven't even known her for that long. She's just another friend. She'll be gone soon, just like all the others.' Bryan thought.

But she was somehow different. He had never felt this way towards anyone before. Whenever she was around Bryan felt happy and everything she said was enjoyable to listen to. Nothing that came out of her mouth was boring, even the things that were repeated.

Whenever she was not around, Bryan wanted to see her. Even right now, even with the anger he had towards her for bringing up this topic, he wanted to see her and just talk like they used to. Bryan missed the days when he would be with her for the meals and sometimes even the outdoor period. But now he just couldn't get the courage to go to her without having an actual answer.

And right now, he just couldn't find one. He simply wanted both of them too much. But then again, he would get to an actual answer when he actually got there. He didn't need one now. He still had a full week and it would be easier to come to a decision when he could actually see what the second choice would be. He had to experience what it would be to choose Jennifer over the injection and his dreams before he could actually arrive at an answer.

Besides, Bryan was beginning to go a bit crazy without seeing Jennifer for over a month. He would do anything right now to spend a little time with her. Maybe then, he wouldn't regret it when he actually chooses the injection.

Bryan couldn't believe it took him one whole month to think of this brilliant plan. He decided to act it out the next day, first thing in the morning. That night was the best sleep Bryan had had in a while.

Chapter 11

As soon as he woke up, Bryan got up and walked over to the bookshelf. He tip-toed across the room making sure he was not waking any of the others up. Everything that day was a joy for Bryan. He would later meet Jennifer for the first time in a month and that just made everything all the more enjoyable.

Even looking at the clock was fun for Bryan.

Bryan looked at the clock, noticing every little detail of the metal cage and its red and round paraphernalia. On it, the long hand of the clock was pointing up as the shorter hand was pointing downward, creating an undisturbed line that divided the clock as a whole.

All the books that were available on the shelf overwhelmed Bryan. Unlike the day he arrived in the camp however, Bryan actually knew the varieties of books available now, and he had a vision in his mind of the type of book he enjoyed the most.

All types of books: mystery, adventure, romance, and even comedy were lying in front of him just waiting for his decision. Bryan took the time to go through every book from left to right, always pausing to look at the front cover.

He looked at the covers closely, and if he liked them, he even went through the trouble of reading the blurbs on the back of each book.

Every single book he chose to read the blurb of had pretty much the same things written on them.

"Riveting!"

"Breathless"

Comments like these were clich?s Bryan had seen in every book he'd ever read, but today he was naive enough to believe it. He piled up all the books that had these clich?s in the back and the pile just kept getting bigger until the loud bell rang announcing that it was time for breakfast.

Bryan got up and carried the huge pile of books that he'd compiled over the hour and a half period he'd spent in front of the bookshelf. The time had passed by very quickly to Bryan's eyes but for the others in the room who'd had to endure Bryan's clanging and banging of books, it'd been a nightmare.

Bryan followed the group down to the main building of the San camp. As usual, he turned right into the hall as the other group of the lucky people turned left. The mere thought of having to give that up gave him shivers. Good thing, Bryan thought, that he had one more week to think it over. He didn't want to make a mistake that he would regret for the rest of his life. But for now, he had to tell Jennifer that he was going to choose her over the injection.

Jennifer's expression as Bryan told her the good news was just what Bryan was expecting. She jumped up from her seat and hugged him. Bryan was glad he'd told her that way.

"That's so great!" She said. Bryan didn't pay attention as Jennifer went on about how she was so glad to have him back and that she'd been so bored without him. Bryan didn't care what she was saying right now. He was just happy that he was having breakfast with her again.

But everything came to a halt when she said, "Now we can get out of here."

Bryan had not expected this. He just thought that he would tell her what she wanted to hear and that would be that. He had never thought beyond that. Now, he was in trouble.

The bell rang, announcing the end of breakfast and Jennifer left the room with one final sentence, "See you later." She had no idea what was going on in Bryan's head at that moment.

What was he going to do? There was no way of procrastinating his way out of this one. He had to make a choice now. The nightmare that Bryan thought he'd dealt with just moments ago was back again.

The time between breakfast and lunch went by quickly. As he had the past month, Bryan just sat on his bed and stared out into nothingness. His head was again racing to find a quick answer to this crisis. He knew he wasn't ready to find an answer to the other question but rather; he just wanted to get away from this. He just wanted both to last. But if he messed up, it was possible he'd have to miss something he wanted because of a simple act of procrastination. At that moment a sudden loud bell interrupted his thoughts, and Bryan mindlessly followed the crowd to lunch. Bryan still wanted to be with Jennifer, no matter how much this troubled him.

During lunch, Bryan just sat next to Jennifer and stared out into open space. Jennifer kept talking and talking next to him but none of the words stuck, only the ones she said during breakfast, "Now let's get out of here."

These words echoed through Bryan's head and soon, lunch was over. Jennifer got up from her seat as if she did not notice Bryan's absent mindedness and told Bryan to his face, "We're going to leave during the outside period. I'll meet you at the center of the giant area." Then, noticing that Bryan was not listening, she said again, "Just come out to the place during the outside time." and she left.

Bryan went back to his bed and kept staring out into nowhere. A train of ideas hit him one by one but none of them seemed to work out perfectly.

He had to show up or else he might not be able to see Jennifer again. Nor could he just tell Jennifer that he wanted to get the injection; she would probably get mad and leave him. Bryan did not want to make Jennifer mad. But Bryan could not give up his childhood dream either.

Without any thought, Bryan's body involuntarily got up at three o'clock and he walked out the door towards the open area where other soldiers roamed about.

He met Jennifer in the center and with her, he headed straight towards the main gate, the same gate Bryan had so enthusiastically entered through just a few months before. Next to the gate was the metal container box.

As Bryan and Jennifer approached the gate, a

group of Sun Worshipers ran over to stop them. All of them formed a wall in front of the gate and surrounded Jennifer and Bryan. One last person came out of the container box and through the crowd towards the two. It was the same person who had "greeted" Bryan when he'd arrived there.

"You can't leave now." The San said.

"Why not? We don't want to take the injection anymore!" Jennifer retorted angrily.

"Not take the vaccine?" the man said, laughing mockingly. "You just can't leave." He gestured for the other Sun Worshipers, " Escort these two back to their cabins."

As the words ended, the other surrounding Sun Worshipers took Jennifer and Bryan by the arms and flew swiftly across the field, taking each of them to their designated bunks.

Bryan did not know exactly why they were treated this way but it was not a bad thing as far as he was concerned. Now, Bryan got to keep both Jennifer and the vaccine. He got to stay with Jennifer for one more week and he would have to take the vaccine. After that, he thought he could figure something out later.

During dinner that evening, Jennifer did not say much but Bryan let her be. He understood what was wrong because he had done the same for the last month. He just figured she had something to think about.

Right as the bell rang announcing the end of the meal, she said, "I will figure out some way to get out of here. I don't understand why they stopped us but don't worry. We will be out of here before you turn."

Bryan didn't let this get to him any more. He knew now that it was close to impossible for her to figure out a way to escape from there. It was perfect. But still, he had to choose before his turn arrived if he wanted to get the injection or not. Jennifer did not know this and Bryan was most likely going to choose the injection anyways, but still, he had to make sure.

But Bryan kept procrastinating on his choice. He kept saying, "Just one more day with Jennifer and I can probably stop."

"Just one more day," became his mantra, as did "I still have that much time." And everyday, he was reminded by the group in front of him being taken for the injection, groups now made up of people from his own cabin, led to the other hallway as the bright light shined out from the ajar door.

One by one, the bunks that surrounded Bryan's were emptied until at last Bryan was left alone, with only nine other people.

The day the bunk next to the bookshelf was empty, Bryan fought over it with the others and took the bunk for his own. He wanted to be able to get more books without disturbing others as he did so.

But mostly, everything was back to normal. Bryan knew this normality would not last long due to the fact that his due date was fast approaching. But Bryan still neglected to choose. Mostly, though, he knew what he wanted. He wanted the injection more than anything he'd ever wanted. But whenever he saw Jennifer, his longing for the injection blurred and that made his decision that much harder. At the same time, he knew that there was no way for Jennifer to take him and escape from this place without the injection and that made Bryan's thought process much simpler. At least he didn't have to choose one thing over the other, and he could tell himself later that he had no other choice.

But just in case, he had to make sure.

Soon, his time arrived. Bryan got up from his bed. His heart pounded against his chest like a hammer. He had woken up an hour early that morning because of his anxiety.

Bryan walked around the almost empty room seeing if anyone else was awake. He noticed that all the others were lying on their beds, reading and seeming nervous, much like Bryan was feeling right now. Today was the day he would 'have' to take the injection.

Bryan sat on his bed, reading, and waiting for the bell located atop the door to ring, announcing that it was time for his injection.

As soon as the bell rang, Bryan ran straight to the door, in front of everyone else. The doors split open and behind it appeared a Sun Worshiper wearing the standard green army suit and white band. He stood there looking at a forty-five degree angle up in the air.

The solider did not say anything but stood there for a few moments. Then, wordlessly, he turned and marched out towards the main building. Bryan, having seen the others do this before, followed the soldier down the empty area in the middle and into the main building.

Bryan glimpsed the rest of the people peeking towards him and the group behind him in awe and jealousy and felt a bit of pride at getting to become the higher species before them. But amongst those groups of people that peeked in envy, Bryan found Jennifer frowning, almost crying as she saw Bryan walking proudly towards the end of their friendship.

Bryan walked into the building and for the first time, he turned left and into the bright, white, shining hallway and into the shining room he had always been so curious about.

But different from his imagination, the door led them to another hallway. At the end of this long hall was a green painted door with a yellow sign on it saying, "Warning! Patients and doctors only," in bold, black letters. At once, Bryan knew that that door was where the people got the injections.

Next to the door was a line of chairs pushed up against the wall and next to the chairs was another door. The soldier led Bryan and the others in through the door and locked it behind them.

The soldier sat the people down around a long table much like the one in the eating room, except here, the table was covered in cloth and there was nothing on top of it. As soon as the door closed, the soldier started talking. Bryan noticed that he talked very unnaturally, as if he'd had to memorize the whole speech.

"Today, you will be injected with the N1E3 vaccine and you will no longer be the ape-like human selves you are now. So, to commemorate this day, we will give you a last meal. You will no longer need to eat when you get this injection."

As this speech came to an end, a line of other soldiers came in through another door on the other side of the room, each holding a metal tray. They put the tray down gently on the table and took the cover off showing what lay on it.

Inside each and every tray there lay foods that Bryan had never seen before. The others in the group seemed to recognize these foods and called it by names Bryan was familiar with, but which left him unable to see the similarity between the packaged hotdogs he'd had before and these trays full of actually delicious looking foods. They did not even seem to have been packaged, ever, lacking the same bitter smell the packaged ones did.

Without hesitation, Bryan and the others started stuffing their mouths with the foods that were put in front of them. The pile of food, however, did not seem to shrink no matter how much he grabbed from it. He ate until he could barely breath, and then after a few moments to catch his breath he ate some more. When he wanted something on the other side of the table, he did not ask. He merely reached across the table and fought for it. If he wanted it, he thought, he needed to get it. After all, he was going to be a San. There were no manners then.

After almost an hour of stuffing himself with food, the soldier that led him here in the first place opened the door and pointed for the group to sit on the chairs next to the injection door.

Bryan, once again, ran towards the chair to take the first spot. He almost threw up on the way. He sat down and waited. Inside the door, Bryan could hear a bunch of clinking and foot steps. These were the same sounds he had heard as he'd waited for his injection when he was thirteen.

Chapter 12

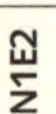

Bryan heard the loud slamming of a door. Then he heard foot steps, immediately thinking them to be the sounds of Sans coming to give him his injection. He could hardly wait. Bryan's legs twitched and he clenched his hands together in anticipation.

Suddenly, Bryan heard a series of loud cracking noises and along with it, a chorus of screams coming from the door at the other end of the hall. Those weren't the noises he was expecting to hear.

Bryan ran down the hall to see what it was. This time, nobody stopped him. He got to the door and grabbed the knob. He held it lightly to make sure the door wouldn't slide open too far when he peered through the crack, and then he got into a comfortable position where he could see what was going on outside.

He peeked through the crack without expecting much, but still being cautious. Through the door, to his surprise, he could see figures in black garments holding small dark boxes that shot little spits of fire everywhere. These people in black seemed like soldiers and were moving very stealthily through the halls. They divided into many groups, while one stayed near the main entrance, and then another group came in from the right hall holding humans by the arms.

Even in the midst of all these things, Bryan could only think about the injection and marveled that the humans were still eating breakfast while this was going on. He had not even the slightest clue of what was going to happen next.

From the same hallway the group of black figures had come from, a large mob of people ran out screaming.

The black figures tried to control these people but couldn't. More and more black figures entered the room as the main part of the building fell more and more into a chaotic state.

The black figures moved around the main area as humans and even Sun Worshipers ran around in chaos.

All the while, the black figures kept grabbing humans by the arms and pulling them away.

Bryan now watched in fear at what was happening. He could feel the chaos in the air even from his position in the hallway. He felt even luckier to be there. He felt lucky to be in a safe place.

Then, a group of Sun Worshiper soldiers flew towards the black figures. The Sun Worshipers flew with great velocity but Bryan still caught a quick glimpse of the expressions on their faces. They seemed angry, angrier than Bryan had ever seen them. All the while, the black figures shot at the Sans in vain as they approached them. Just as they were going to reach them, someone screamed at Bryan.

"Hey! What are you doing? Get down here, you're first."

Bryan turned around quickly in surprise. He saw two Sun Worshipers sticking their heads out of the injection room door with annoyance on their faces. Just then Bryan heard a scream which sounded something like "Paul."

'Who's Paul?' Bryan thought. But he did not budge from that spot. He was too intrigued by what was going on outside.

The two Sun Worshipers wearing white gowns flew down the hall and grabbed Bryan by the arms, dragging him down the hallway like a corpse. Just then, the door at the end of the hall slammed open and a group of four or five black-garbed figures ran through the door holding the fire-spitting boxes and shooting them at Bryan.

He felt the grips of the two people holding him loosen. He looked up to see what had happened, only to see the two Sun Worshipers fall to the ground bleeding. On their necks were holes the size of quarters and from them, blood was spurting out like a fountain. The Sans did not twist and turn in pain, and it was clear that they were dead. Bryan carefully moved the arms of the dead men off of him and got to his feet.

He shivered in disgust at the mere thought of having not one but two dead Sans holding him. He wiped his hands on his clothes, and stared at the corpses in awe. This was the first time he had seen any San fall.

But slowly, Bryan could see that the holes were sealing. Little by little the edges of the wounds were coming together and he could see a metallic thing as big as a coin slowly creeping out from inside the hole.

Bryan could not help himself from being scared. The story he had been intrigued by and interested in just a few seconds ago had just become far too real. What he thought would never happen to him, was happening to him right now.

He knew the Sans would be very angry when they

got up. Like the coward he was, Bryan ran towards a corner and hid behind the other waiting people for the injection. He didn't want to be a part of this fight between two great powers like that: Two Sans and five people, people with the capability to knock a San to the ground for long minutes.

"These black suited people must be strong," he thought.

Bryan then heard a familiar voice, screaming. The sound was distant, dulled by the combat outside and the roar of adrenaline in his blood, but Bryan could make out that it was Jennifer's voice. He turned and saw that there was Jennifer, standing behind the black figures. Bryan instinctively shouted back, "Hey! Get away from them! They're dangerous!"

But Jennifer did not budge, she kept screaming at Bryan something he couldn't understand. He was too scared. All the sounds surrounding him had coalesced into one large and incomprehensible chorus and above it, there was only the pounding of his own heart.

Bryan could see Jennifer waving her hands. Her mouth kept moving but what Bryan heard from it was nothing he could understand. From her motions and expressions however, he could guess. It seemed as though she wanted help, and though Bryan wanted to, he was too scared for himself to do anything. His body did not listen to any of his commands. His legs were glued to the ground and he couldn't move. After countless efforts in trying to make himself move towards Jennfier, finally, involuntarily, as if someone had taken over his very body, Bryan got up from his crouching position behind the others. But his body wouldn't listen from there on. That was his limit.

Bryan couldn't reply, and was ashamed of himself for being such a coward. But what could he do? He was only human. That's why he was there in the first place.

He could still see Jennifer screaming and screaming until at last the group of black-garbed figures pulled her back out to the main part of the building. She reached out her hand towards Bryan as she vanished, but he stood there petrified. He didn't know what to do.

He wanted to help Jennifer, but his mind and intentions were all towards the injection and saving his own life. Now he knew it was now or never. The black figures were probably going to burn down the camp, so either one way or another. Bryan had to choose now. He would not be able to have either choice if he chose wrong now.

Chapter 13

Meanwhile, outside, everything was going crazy. Every single human left was now out of their cabin, and were either screaming and running or lying on the ground lifeless and dead. It was a catastrophe.

The cement ground was covered with blood and one could not take a step without finding a puddle of some type of bodily fluid. This included vomit and urine, but mostly blood.

As the humans were running around trying to save themselves, the black figures and Sun Worshipers seemed to be more interested in killing one another than the mad rabble of humans. However, many of the black figures seemed to also be trying to grab humans and put them onto a large metal machine. This was where Jennifer was being taken as well.

Instinctively, the humans tried to run away. And by doing this, they were being shot at unintentionally. The black figures would shoot at a San, only to accidentally hit humans.

In the middle of the chaos there was a set of large metal things, each looking much like an automobile, except with wings. One was floating in the air and from it jumped rows and rows of black figures, all armed with a shooting box. In the air there were five more large metal things floating above ground waiting for a spot to land.

And in front of all the troops, there stood one person leading the way. She shouted words of leadership in a commanding and stern voice, something which stood in marked contrast to her facial features. She too had black apparel on and held a metal box like all the other black-garbed figures. Around her neck was a slim cord with a pair of sunglasses hanging at the end of it. On her head was a black hat that was shaped like a bun. She was in fact the woman Bryan had met at the antique shop.

"Charge! This is a rescue mission. Don't shoot unless attacked. Just in and out! Grab as many survivors as you can and go!" She said. "We can't risk too many soldiers.”

The black figures all shouted at once “Yes sir!”

The black figures separated and each group of three ran into a cabin. The remaining ten or so black-garbed attackers ran into the main building, holding their cracking boxes up high. The leader followed them in,

“Hey Jack, you got my back right?” One of them said to the other. He was obviously scared.

“Of course Paul, I’m your friend.” Jack answered. “Hey, don’t be scared. We’re not going to die. These guys don’t even have guns. They’re just strong and heal real fast. We can beat them.” It was evident that he wanted to help his friend but that he was scared as well.

Just then, Jack and Paul saw something green pass by them extremely fast. Along with it, they heard a sound much like the wind.

“Hey you see that?” Jack said.

“Ye....” Paul started but he suddenly disappeared along with a short yelp of pain.

All around the room there splashed something red, as if someone had ripped open a big bottle of red paint in the room and then on the floor landed the torn and ragged pieces of an almost unidentifiable Paul.

“Paul!”

Every other black figure turned their head in

disgust, including the woman leading them. Jack stood there, staring at the corpse in growing astonishment and anger. All of it had happened so fast. He started screaming and brought the metal box up, beginning to shoot everywhere in the room. He didn't aim anywhere in particular but instead just shot to hit something, anything, the thing that took his friend.

All around the room, there were suddenly holes and burning marks along the walls and the cracking noise was so deafening, even the black-garbed figures grabbed at their ears. And then, the shooting came to a sudden halt as the leader grabbed the man's shoulder.

"You can't get him back that way, Jack," she said.

Jack fell to the ground and started crying. He had just lost his lifelong best friend.

Chapter 14

Bryan watched as the black figures pulled Jennifer out the door and the rest jogged over towards him and the other humans. He could not move his body; he was just too scared.

He was still in the corner between the door and the chairs behind the other people. He had just stood there for long minutes, not doing anything.

And there, just in front of him, the two fallen Sans were getting to their feet. They were a little shaken but the holes in their necks were gone. They slowly shook their heads, looking around to make sure everything was okay.

The other humans by that point had already pushed Bryan out of that corner and taken it for themselves. Bryan was in the middle of the hallway now, trapped between the two opponents, simply standing there. He couldn't even think about moving out of the way.

The two Sans were perfect again, back to normal and about to take off towards the black-garbed figures. Just as they leaped into the air, the black figures shot at them again.

This time, they missed. But they did hit something. Bryan felt a sharp pain biting at his left arm. He looked down and saw that there was a large hole in his upper left arm. Bryan grabbed at it and screamed, the agony just beginning to hit him. This was the most pain he had ever been through in this life. He'd broken bones been bruised many times before, but nothing like this. Bryan fell to his knees and kept screaming in pain.

The two Sans swept into the group of attackers with extreme velocity. The white gowns they'd been wearing flew off when they leapt and were now flapping in the air. Down the hall, the Sans reached the first black-garbed figure before the gowns had even landed on the ground

The rest of the attackers shot at them with greater urgency but less accuracy, and swiftly the two Sans took the first man out. The rest in the group continued to shoot as the two Sun worshipers charged them. Another of the black figures was injured in the very moment another shouted for them to retreat.

"Pull back!" she shouted. Bryan was unable to hear exactly what she said, but once again, he recognized her voice from the antique shop.

'What was she doing here with the enemy?' He thought.

The people ran out the door and the two Sans turned back towards Bryan. Their bodies were covered with holes as big as the ones they'd had in their necks, and from each wound there was blood pouring.

But unlike before, they did not fall to the ground. Instead they limped over towards Bryan, slowly at first but beginning to gather speed. Now was his chance, Bryan knew. The Sans were injured and if he wanted to get to Jennifer now, he might be able to escape. He had seen what had happened to these Sans just a few moments ago. It had taken them a good five minutes to recover from being shot. Bryan calculated in his head that that gave him about two or three minutes to choose. Even if they reached him, he would be able to run away due to their injuries. But Bryan knew, he was injured as well.

His left arm still felt like it was burning and the blood kept pouring out. He felt lightheaded and he wanted nothing so much as to go to sleep now. But all he could think about was if he was this hurt, what could have happened to Jennifer?

The Sans approached and Bryan accidentally made eye contact with one of them. They glared at him in fury, spitting blood on the ground in disgust and anger. Bryan felt a trickle of water move down his pants in response, and there at his feet he could see a shallow puddle of yellow urine forming, spreading over the ground until it mixed with a puddle of blood.

Everything slowed down. He could hear his heart beat against his chest more distinctly now and everything around him seemed to move in slower and slower motion. His body felt numb and his arm was no longer hurting. He could hear a mash of sounds from outside the door, the sounds of people screaming and the cracking from the fire-boxes.

Bryan did not know if this change was from the adrenaline rush or from the loss of blood but what he did know was that he could take advantage of the sudden numbness as a chance to run away. He could go save Jennifer.

Bryan got to his feet. He made sure his legs weren't too weak to run, or at least limp, and when he was about to take off for Jennifer, one thought hit him like a hammer.

'Why should I?'

This thought left him rigid and unmoving.

He knew Jennifer was his friend and he cared for her very much but why did it matter? In front of him, literally in front of him, was a door that could lead him to the life he wanted. This was no longer a dream or a nightmare; he was actually here. He'd witnessed the deaths of two people today just because they were trying to stop this organization.

He knew the reality before him was legitimate. He'd even heard a Sun Worshiper soldier say it. He could quote him right now.

The soldier had said, not even an hour ago, "Today, you will be injected with the N1E3 vaccine and you will no longer be the ape-like humans you are now". Then he'd even eaten his last meal. Bryan could still taste the delicious hotdogs on his breath.

He didn't want to give up something right there in front of him for some girl.

But he also knew if he didn't go help Jennifer now, she might die. He would no longer be able to see her, ever again. Maybe not even her body. Bryan would fly around not even remembering her. And it wouldn't even matter then because Bryan wouldn't be able to feel sadness....but until then, his heart would feel as though it were broken apart, ripped into pieces.

For another month or so, just like Bob, he knew that he would feel human emotions. Bob had felt sympathy and compassion towards Bryan, but when the drug had finally and fully worked on him, he'd forgotten it all. And until that point, Bryan would miss Jennifer.

Bryan could remember her facial expression and her screaming when she was being pulled away. She was definitely scared. She'd probably been asking for Bryan's help in saving her life. But Bryan ignored her completely. He'd been scared for himself while he was safe with the Sans half dead, lying behind him. She on the other hand, she'd been pulled away by the very people that had made the Sans that way in the first place, probably being taken to her death.

Bryan felt guilt and anger towards himself for being so selfish then. How could he think of himself when his only friend, one that he loved, was being pulled away to be killed like that?

Bryan then understood what the characters in the books were feeling when they loved another person of the opposite gender very much. He felt exactly the same way they described. He loved Jennifer. But that didn't make much of a difference. He knew that he had just let her die.

'Why can't I be brave like those guys in the stories?' he thought to himself and stared blankly at the half dead souls behind him in shame.

He knew he should leave now while he had the

chance to go help Jennifer. If he didn't, he might not be able to see her ever again. He would never be able to say what he felt towards her.

'But' Bryan thought again. This was no longer a fantasy from one of the books he was always reading. This was real life. In the books the characters could do anything because it was all made up, but it was different for Bryan. He would only get one life, and did he really want to give that power up just for a girlfriend? Once he got the injection, he knew he would never need her again.

No matter how pretty or nice she was, she would never be able to give him what the injection could. The injection offered power, money and the respect of others. What could Jennifer give him? A broken arm, an entire life of living incognito, and maybe death?

Life wasn't like the books, and you couldn't just start reading another one when you weren't happy with your choice. This life was the only 'book' he would ever get, and there was no turning back once he flipped the page. This was it. It was now or never.

In frustration, Bryan struggled to find an excuse for himself, just one thing that would allow him to feel better; one lousy excuse that would keep him from wanting to kill himself for making the wrong decision. And just then, another thought hit him.

'If I go now to help Jennifer, we will probably

both die. But if I get the injection first, I will probably be able to fight them off and this arm will be healed. I can get both. I need both.' But deep down, he knew just as well that this was merely a lie that he told himself to satisfy his greed without feeling any guilt.

Bryan chose just in time, for the two Sans were back to their full strength and were now next to Bryan. He did not hesitate to follow them nor did they pull him forcefully into the injection room.

Bryan walked in by his own choice and sat down on the chair as the two stood by on either side. There were lights everywhere, both next to him and above him, lights that blinded him with a harsh and unforgiving glare. All over the walls were white tiles that made the room even brighter, forcing Bryan to squint, barely allowing him to see anything. The two Sans leaned in front of him, the glare of light and shadow making it difficult to see their faces.

"Tape him down," one said.

"Hey, did you hear?" the other asked as he taped Bryan's arms and torso down to the chair.

"What?" the first one asked, and Bryan could tell that this person was not happy or excited to hear what was coming next.

"This kid's the one Bob brought in. Remember? The one who thought Bob was the guy who'd gotten beaten up?" This person was evidently very interested in what he was saying.

"Really?" said the first, and started laughing.

"Yeah, this is the one. He even slept in his house and everything. Then Bob took advantage of that and went along with the lie. Well, that's what he was trained to do."

Bryan then realized what was going on. He understood what Jennifer had been screaming at him and why the guards had not let him leave. But he was too late. The injection had already been put in him. He strained against his bonds futilely, already growing weaker.

Bob had been a propaganda effort by the Sun Worshipers to gather people into this camp. And the camp was in truth nothing but a death camp for all humans. Bryan would then have given anything for his old, worthless life back.

If only, he thought, his vision fading, he hadn't been so selfish. And with that, his eyes fluttered close and he fell into an eternal sleep.

Chapter 15

As the black figures pulled Jennifer out the door, she screamed out loud to Bryan, wishing he would now come dashing out the gate so they could leave together. She didn't want to go by herself, when she knew Bryan would have to die. She couldn't believe Bryan had not listened to her when she called for him just a few seconds ago.

"Bryan! Let's go! It's a trap! That's not the injection!" She screamed. She jumped up and down waving her hands for him to run away while he could.

She pulled away her arms as the human soldiers behind her grabbed at her. She wanted to run down and bring Bryan back herself but the soldiers would not let her.

"We'll get him, ma'am, get to the helicopter. Don't worry," they shouted, but she couldn't trust them. She didn't even know what a "helicopter" was. But there, even when she was screaming her head off, Bryan seemed not to hear her. His eyes seemed to have lost focus on the world and he was just standing there, staring at her, confused.

Jennifer kept fighting the soldiers wearing black off until the point Bryan just ran off and hid in the corner. That action broke Jennifer's heart, and tears suddenly ran down her face. Not tears of disappointment for Bryan not listening to her, but simply tears from knowing that if he hid like that, he was going to die.

She stopped fighting off the black-garbed figures and was pulled away listlessly, like a dead body, no longer screaming, no longer trying to say anything at all. But just as she was pulled out the door, she took one last effort to bring Bryan to her, screaming out to him with the last of her strength. Through the closing door, she could see the human soldiers cautiously approaching the dead Sans, the humans gathered in fear, and behind them all, she could see Bryan, crunched up into a ball in the corner, hiding. More tears dropped from her eyes as she said, quietly to her self, "Good bye."

She knew at that moment that that would be the last time she would ever see Bryan. She would never be able to see her best and only friend ever again.

"We'll bring you to the helicopter." Said one of the figures. "You just have to stay there for a while and wait. And soon, we will bring some more humans and we will head back to the human base."

The black figures told her more then, but she didn't pay attention.

Chapter 16

Five hundred years ago, when the injection was supposedly made, the world was peaceful. Everyone was human and there was no discrimination of any type among the people of the world. None of what Bryan believed was true. There had been no economical break down.

What had been thought of as a way to save mankind was actually only a military experiment to create soldiers. John Servodeus Jr. had been the head of this research and had been very enthusiastic about it. The project was a precaution, an effort to create a new breed of better soldiers for the inevitable day when war broke out.

The way the great savior John Servodeus Jr. was portrayed was not remotely close to reality. He was not trying to save the world from mass destruction nor was he even caring enough to even give the world a thought when making his drug. He was merely trying to find a way to take power, and to stand above other men. Desperately, he'd sought the means to that end.

On June 19, 2131, the N1E2 was created. Without any hesitation, John Sercodeus tested the drug on himself. Surprisingly, he received the powers he desired and soon after the others who were part of that research were likewise given the same dose. They had become powerful, and they did not see the side effects.

Soon after, this group believed they could rule the world. They were all very strong, no longer had to eat, and could heal rapidly. And just like these scientists, the soldiers of the world wished to receive the injection as well. The military had yet to find the side effects of the drug, and so kept the funding going towards the doctor's "great" experiment.

Soon, military personal everywhere had received the drug and even common citizens were beginning to long for its gifts. People now wanted the same power that some of their friends, family or even acquaintances had. One by one, people began to join the army to get this drug and the number of SANS (Supernatural

American National Soldiers) upon the American continent grew exceedingly large.

By 2134, nearly half the population of the United States of America was composed of Sans. But at the same time, the side effects were beginning to kick in.

The people who had received the drug in the year 2131 were beginning to act overly aggressive and even violent. Their morality and sense of ethics were dulled, and their belief in themselves as a better human being was no longer a patriotic catchphrase but rather seen as being nothing less than the truth. The Homo Sanus (derived actually from the SANS but later put together as Sanus for propaganda purposes) was now the better, stronger healthier version of the Homo Sapien, and it soon became common thought that anyone who wasn't injected was worth little indeed.

Soon, one by one, cults of delusional Sans were congregating and worshiping John Servodeus Jr. as their "God or creator", their messiah and leader. These cults then coalesced into one giant conglomerate of a following who all believed in one sole scripture:

"Humans are worse than Sans."

And these people followed this law to the letter. They started to accumulate, attacking and sometimes killing innocent humans all around the United Sates. These cults called themselves the Sun Worshipers, and thus John Servodeus Jr. achieved his dream of becoming all-powerful. He had become the leader and god of the most powerful cult in the world.

In the following year, the number of Sans beginning to show side effects multiplied and joined the group of Sun Worshipers. One by one the Sun Worshipers then began to destroy cities and states which would not kneel to them, and in that struggle many lives were taken. There was no longer a national military or government to protect the people, for the Sun Worshipers themselves were those people. As for the rest of the world, they too were too late in realizing that they should have done more to save the continent.

Victorious, the Sun worshipers had next headed south towards Mexico, seeking to dominate other nearby countries. What had started out as a nation's experiment in military precaution had turned into a worldwide epidemic spread by people through the use of needles and drugs.

Other countries in the world took heed then, and thankfully for the humans, the allies of the United States of America came into the country and fought for those who remained. Working together not as a gathering of nations of different ethnic and racial background but rather a gathering of one unified species, the human race was at last brought together by the threat of a common enemy.

A war between humans and Sans was declared,

and there were many casualties on both sides. The Sans believed it un-San to use manmade weapons and instead fought only with their physical advantages. This gave the humans a slight advantage because of the guns and firearms that protected them. The truth was however, that the humans had two advantages over Sans, one that they had weapons, and the second being that they did not lose control of their common sense through unreasonable self ego.

However, at the same time, the Sans possessed the ability to almost miraculously recover from the gravest of wounds, and were many times stronger than a human. They actually had the right to possess their almost maniacally egotistical mindset. They could go against the human armies without anything but their own hands, and they were without a doubt a physically better species.

This led in time to a stalemate between the two species, as both had advantages against the other and thus neither could win completely. The leaders of the humans and John Servodeus Jr., the leader of the Sans, met together and worked to create a peace treaty.

This treaty had only two rules.

The first was that neither side would ever again cross over to the other side of the world. The Eastern hemisphere, including Eurasia and Africa, was now solely the realm of the humans, while the Americas were formally recognized as belonging to the Sans.

The humans left the American continents, and in their absence the Sun worshipers worked to make a society of their own. The war which had led to the founding of San civilization was well known, but was considered embarrassing considering the fact that the Sans had been unable to defeat the humans. Therefore, no San talked about it. For the first hundred years or so, it was simply left as an unspoken embarrassment, but in time the Sun Worshipers crafted a new history to cover up the event, and it was that carefully crafted lie which was celebrated every year.

Time passed, and the world was slowly molded back into shape. The damage from the wars was soon repaired by the super human society, and at last life began to move on. The generations that followed did not know what had happened in the war, nor even the fact that there had been a war. San civilization grew, and lacking empathy or love, people began discarding their children, feeling no parental attachments. Orphanages were quickly built for the discarded San babies, and with reluctance, another was built for the humans when it was discovered that they were capable of being turned into a San when they hit puberty.

The descendants of all were never taught what really happened on June 19, 2131. and so, it was forgotten until today.

What Bryan and all others had thought to be true all their life, was in fact nothing more than a lie made by the Sun Worshipers as a way to take power.

Chapter 17

The short walk across the outside area, which Jennifer had experienced many times before, now felt terribly long. The short ten yards to the helicopter felt like miles instead, and the fact that all around her were dead bodies and bleeding people made the situation all the worse. In all directions, high-pitched screams yelling for help filled the air along with fierce growls from Sun Worshipers.

On one side, there was a pile of dead black-garbed soldiers, all being carried away by other wounded souls. The wounded were all but dead themselves and screaming in agony as they struggled to pull away the dead bodies. On the other were Sans, wounded but healing, growling at their enemies and gathering strength. They were drooling blood and showed their teeth like a pack of angry wolves ready to get at their prey.

The uniforms of the Sun Worshipers were ripped apart and blood covered them head to toe, but where the blood could be seen, there were no wounds. Their green skin lay there beneath the garments, unmarked, ready to fight. It was a horrible comparison to the half-dead soldiers of the other side, some of whom were already a few yards in front of Jennifer, limping for safety. Jennifer winced in disgust as a soldiers in black limped by, dragging their right foot behind them, the limb twisted all the way around in the wrong direction.

The horrible truth was that no matter how much one shot at the Sans, they would get up. They would always get up. Further, the more they were shot, the faster they seemed to heal, their adrenaline increasing their strengths as they grew ever more vicious, ever more angry.

The only ones that weren't healing were the ones that were somehow unfortunate enough to be shot directly in the head. There was a few that were lying on the ground this way but the rest, they would just get angrier and angrier until the human who'd shot them in the first place was dead by their hands.

The Sun Worshipers growled louder as Jennifer ran towards the helicopter with the other humans while the soldiers tried to stop the Sun Worshipers from coming any nearer. The loud gun shots from the little machines nearly deafened Jennifer, except she could hear a loud, high pitched beep that could be overheard over even the loudest gun shots.

Suddenly, a person next to her fell to the ground, dead. At first, she thought that he had been shot by one of the human soldiers, but when she looked down, she could see that above the body's shoulders, there was nothing. The act of a Sun worshiper. Now, overwhelmed with fear, her heart pumped faster and faster and without any thought, she kept running for safety. The only way she would survive this, she thought, was by getting to the machine thing. Bryan was not even in her thoughts anymore, as she had to worry for herself now and didn't have enough time to have anyone else in her thoughts.

She ran and ran towards the aircraft while it was still hovering. She didn't care if she fell and hurt herself, she just didn't want her head to get ripped off. When she got to the flying vehicle, she jumped on, not caring if she tripped or not. Once inside she sat on the seat and resisted the temptation of slamming the door close. Instead she waved for the others to quickly get there so that they could flee. Without waiting much longer, she began to shut the door.

"Hurry up!" She screamed as she pulled the door half shut and moved all the way to the back of the vessel, hoping then that the Sun Worshipers would not be able to get at her. That was the first thing she had ever said to a human, other than Bryan. "Hurry up."

The soldiers and human fugitives ran towards the helicopter with great speed, but one by one, the fugitives at the rear were swept up into the air and ripped apart like paper.

By then, they'd reached the aircraft and only three people were left, including the human soldiers. The soldiers carefully herded the people through the space Jennifer had left in the doorway, at last allowing it to be closed. Jennifer finally felt safe. She would now no longer have to run for her life, as long as things worked out.

Through the bulletproof window, she peeked out. On the other side, she could see that the black-garbed humans were running back to the main building, one last time. The people who entered never seemed to come out. There was blood on the ground, and Sans in green were seen soaring through the air everywhere.

As Jennifer stared in awe at the brave souls in black, she suddenly saw a flash of black pass by the window. It passed by so quickly that she couldn't tell what it was. She thought it must have been a human soldier being thrown like the others. But just as she finished that thought, a black garbed being glided down from the sky right in front of them. It came closer to the window and looked inside. When Jennifer made eye contact with her, the woman winked and turned around.

The woman stood there for a moment, seemingly in thought, and then took off. She didn't run or jog but simply leaped into the air and flew towards the main building with unbelievable speed.

That person was most definitely a San. But why was she wearing black?

Chapter 18

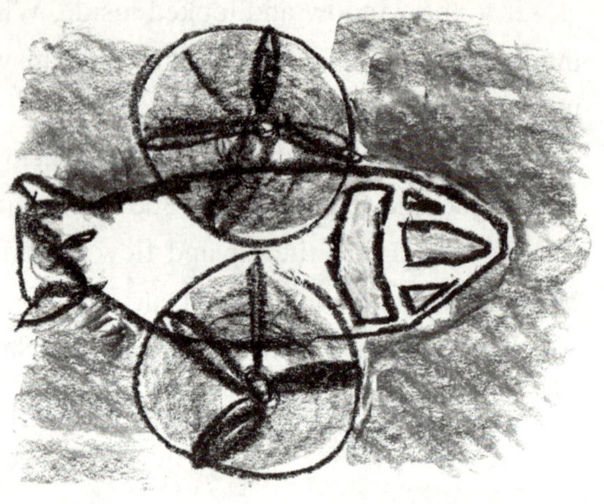

Christina, the San who had helped the humans was in fact the daughter of Mr. Servodeus, the leader of the Sun worshipers. However, although she was part of the Sun Worshipers, she did not believe their ideologies.

Long before, around the time Bryan was born, she had been born as well. By that time, everyone was sent to orphanages, human or San. This was true for Christina as well. She was given the injection, and she was on her way.

When she was about five years old, she had already gotten her full abilities and was thereafter separated from the humans. One day, while playing with her friends and practicing her flight, John Servodeus came into the orphanage and picked her up with his long ape-like arms and carried her out. She was confused and scared for there was band of huge Sun Worshipers guarding John Servodeus.

He gave her his own family name and let her keep the name her real parents had given her. The real parents at first found it irritating for someone to take something that was theirs. This was not out of any parental attachment towards their own daughter but rather a material obsession. They did not like the fact that Servodeus took what was theirs.

However, because of Servodeus's status in the world, he was able to keep the girl as his daughter. The parents were given high positions in the Sun Worshiper society instead, and incomes to match. In addition to this, they were allowed to keep Servodeus's son as their own.

Servodeus had found his own son misfit to him. With a high, distinguished forehead, fat cheeks and a natural obesity, the son looked entirely like his father. Servodeus , however, did not want to believe this and wanted a to claim a better-looking daughter as his own. His ego would not allow the idea that someone like himself would have a child that was anything but beautiful. So, Christina was claimed as a better replica of his own 'handsome' features.

The son was found wanting by the step parents as well. With one look at the child, they threw the boy out, discarding it in an orphanage without even giving him a last name. They would rather have had no child than one as ugly as Servodeus.

On the other hand, Servodeus treated his daughter with great care and taught her many things, things he felt she would need later in life when she inherited the leader position from her father. Servodeus tried his best to show Christina how a leader of the Sun Worshipers should act. Servodeus gave what he could to Christina, a thing that was very close to love in fact, and raised her into one of the most educated and best Sans in the world.

He taught his daughter everything and let her read any books from the Sun Worshiper library. Reading a book a day, no matter how long it was, she learned everything from medicine and how to tend sick humans to even how to kill a human by the time she was fifteen. She soon read every book available to her in the library and was considered one of the most educated Sans alive.

Christina was very smart and understood everything she was taught. But something was very different with her, something that made her different from everyone else in San society. In her brain was a chemical imbalance, and so it was that the injection did not affect her mind in the same way. Where all others had dulled emotions, she did not. Nor did she strongly feel the hate and anger the others did, nor the need to separate the two species.

In other words, she did not hate humans. She felt compassion towards them, and sympathy. She felt they were only less fortunate and deserved more than what they received. Until only a few months before, she'd thought everyone thought as she did. But somehow, her father Servodeus had never learned this. It was the thought that she did not need to show something everyone felt that saved her from the wrath of the rest of the Sun Worshipers.

Until six months ago. At that time, Christina had been going around the city looking for antiques to collect. She had always had a hobby of collecting antiques. That was when she met Bryan. She immediately knew he was human and had felt bad for him. His face had been covered with a dirty green powder and his clothes had been very ragged. On top of this, Bryan seemed overly self-conscious and embarrassed to speak to her. Whenever he spoke, peeking up to make eye contact, he quickly dropped his gaze down again in complete and utter shame.

She'd bought the automobile and left the store. Even when she'd left the store however, she could not stop thinking about how she felt bad for the young man. So she'd returned and decided to follow Bryan. She'd wanted to help him somehow.

But she'd found a group of drunk Sun Worshipers beating Bryan instead. She'd been outnumbered at the time, and she knew the worshipers would not have been able to recognize her even if she barged in. And so she'd hid until the worshipers were done, and then saved Bryan as best she could. She'd carried Bryan to his home and using her learned skills as a doctor, she'd helped him.

When she was finished and finally returned to her own home, Servodeus was waiting. He had already found out about her helping other humans, and so Christina was consequently forced out of her house. When she left her house, she was homeless, and being a San, she had no friends who cared enough for her to help. So she started traveling west. Somewhere where her helping a human would not have been talked about yet.

She'd had to travel all the way to the very tip of the North American continent where people were scarce. There, a small group of Sun worshipers were located and she was able to stay there with them. Their communications had been cut off for the moment due to weather conditions, and they did not even know at first that she was Servodeus's daughter. This was a good thing, for she knew they could not easily be informed of a traitor in their territory.

She hated her father for making her leave her own home just because she had helped a human. She felt that humans had lives too, and that they deserved better. She understood, not through an emotional sense, but through a completely objective point of view, that Sans were not better than humans. If anything, they were less, for they were merely chemically enhanced humans and had been created because of humans. If anything, humans should have been considered the higher race, for they were the ones able to come up with the drug. She also knew from a few books she'd secretly read in the library that Sans were in fact accidents, and that they were supposed to be better than what they were.

With an effort to try to make an ally of her hatred, she started rumors about her father. She spoke to Sans, Sun worshipers, and even humans, anyone she could get a hold of in fact, and told them rumors that had the potential to pull the cult of Sun Worshipers apart. The most effective she thought, was the suggestion that her father was not Sans.

Using her father's abnormal obesity against him, and stressing the fact that the Sans were a species that did not require food, she created the very plausible rumor that her father was human. She told stories of finding her father putting on green makeup in the bathroom, and at that moment understanding that her own father was in fact a human. She explained that that was when she left her house, and that everyone else was too blinded by his status to notice the truth.

No one listened to her however, and soon she was dismissed as either crazy or delusional. No one treated her badly, but they stopped listening to her completely. Finally, when the communication between Servodeus and the distant base she was located in was reestablished, Christina was banned from that region as well.

So, angered at her father, she left the place and started looking for other ways to destroy her father's work in the Sun Worshiper's society. She longed for his position so that she could rule the worshipers better and create a greater, nonviolent world. She kept traveling west towards the ocean, until at last coming across a large metal thing much like the automobile. From it, black figures had emerged.

She had just encountered the humans. They were wearing all black and within an instant, she knew that they must be the humans she'd read about, the species that was surviving on the other side of the Earth. Working with them, she was informed in more depth about the treaty, and in time offered to become a spy. She was no longer able to go back to the Sun

Worshiper bases, but she could still watch the San news and wander their city streets.

It was there that she found out about the human death camp and decided that that would be her chance to become the Sun Worshipers new leader.

Now that the rescue mission was over and the humans were saved, she decided that the angered and confused Sun Worshipers would now be ready to believe anything. All she had to do was deflect the anger for the mysterious black-garbed soldiers back onto Servodeus instead, making them believe that he was actually what they hated most: human.

And so in the end, John Servodeus was not such a bad person, having taught Christina how to think. And that would be the key that would help her defeat him. After all, like humans, Sans were simple beings.

N1E2

초판 1쇄 발행 | 2010년 9월 1일

지은이 | 조동현
표지그림 · 삽화 | 조동현
발행인 | 김영애
디자인 | 서정태

펴낸곳 | 에스엠
등록 | 2007년 10월 1일 제23-4714호
주소 | 서울시 중구 을지로3가 291-45번지
전화 | 02-2279-5033
팩스 | 02-2273-2541

값 | 8,000원
ISBN 978-89-960390-0-6

※잘못된 책은 교환해드립니다